BROADCAST BLOWOUT

Clash to the End

BROADCAST BLOWOUT

Clash to the End

Ken Bosket

ISBN: 9798218917258

Library of Congress Control Number: 2026901927

K&B Information Services Platform

kbosket123@gmail.com

For my wife, Dayema.
Appreciating her patience throughout this journey
and her reminders about the significance of
visualization. It was her support and encouragement
that kept me believing that this book was possible.

The truth erupted in a light.

1

Media Empire

At six foot four and 230 pounds, sporting brown short-cropped hair and a goatee, Mitch has a presence that commands attention. As he prepares to go live, he looks at the clock, which reads 2:59 p.m., and the room falls silent. His producer, Jake, glances at Mitch with a smile, then counts down: Five, four, three, two, one. He points at Mitch through the clear glass separating them, and with a commanding voice, Mitch is on the air.

"Welcome, America! My name is Mitch Corvane, and you're listening to the one and only *Consultant of Conservatism* on WCONS in New York City. For those new to my show and those on the dark side of the world, I'm the top conservative talk show host in the nation, with over three hundred stations broadcasting my show from the ballrooms of New York City to the inner cities of California."

Mitch sits upright in his chair and leans into the microphone.

"Before I continue, let me clarify who I am. I'm a conservative, not a Republican. I do not compromise my beliefs just for the sake of compromise, and the term *moderate* is not in my vocabulary. I stand firmly by strong conservative principles. The legislators currently in office are weak, spineless political hacks who are willing to cater to their opponents to preserve their seats in Congress."

Anger rises and fills the booth as Mitch bangs his fist on the desk.

"I'm frustrated with having to compromise on core issues that form the foundation of the Conservative Party. I'm tired of weak, sycophantic politicians who talk about conservative values but then push moderate policies behind our backs. I'm fed up with officials who appear on my show, thinking they can deceive my informed audience. They say one thing on my program, then go back to their offices and make deals that undermine everything we stand for as conservatives!"

Mitch leans closer to the microphone.

"But wait: As much as I dislike the current officials representing us, I also hate the socialist values of the Liberal Party. This party has Robin Hood syndrome: Rob the rich to give to the poor! This is a party that supports widespread redistribution, cradle-to-grave welfare, unlimited immigration, abortions on demand, and government-run health care!"

Jake signals him to take a break. Seeing this, Mitch gets frustrated and shouts.

"Well, I'm telling all my listeners right now, we'll not tolerate this anymore. We're losing our language! We're losing our culture, and we're losing our faith! This is our country, with our values and traditions. We'll not let a socialist, liberal party destroy the greatest country in the world! We'll be right back."

Jake cuts to a commercial break as he leans back in his chair, smiling at his monitor that shows an array of callers waiting to speak their minds.

Meanwhile, across town, the nation's top syndicated liberal talk show host is ready to go on the air. Paul Vorbont stands about six feet tall and has a slight beer belly. As he enters his studio, he wears his signature tweed jacket with comfortable denim jeans. After pulling his chair into position at his desk, he looks focused, leaning slightly forward toward the microphone.

"America! Welcome to WPROG in New York City. This is Paul Vorbont, the top nationally syndicated liberal talk show host in the country. That's right . . . I said liberal! For those unfamiliar with liberal terminology, I'll provide a brief refresher on some key concepts. Liberals are open-minded, freethinking, and caring Americans who love our country and want to ensure the rights of all Americans are protected, regardless of race, creed, color, or gender."

Paul leans into the microphone as his voice grows louder.

"We believe in an all-inclusive nation and want all Americans to have their place under this tent. We want the government to serve the will of the people, not the interests of corporations. We believe in the right of all Americans to have health care and the right of women to make a choice. We want the race toward the pursuit of happiness to be obtainable for all Americans. We want all immigrants to have the opportunity to achieve the American dream, not just affluent immigrants with political influence and money. What happened to the America that said, 'Give me your tired, your poor, your huddled masses, yearning to breathe free'?"

Paul looks at the clock as his producer, Rochelle, signals for a break.

"Give credit to the Democratic Party. They established the forty-hour workweek, minimum wage laws, and the Civil Rights and Voting Rights acts. They passed the Family and Medical Leave Act, established the GI Bill, and created Social Security and Medicare. It's the Democratic Party that advocates for a ban on assault weapons because these weapons are designed for one purpose: to kill people!"

Paul looks at Rochelle and nods as he lowers his voice.

"As for the opposition party, which demands less government, complains about welfare given to individuals while providing welfare to corporations, fights for the unborn child but limits services that would enable the child to live outside the womb . . ."

Rochelle frantically waves to Paul through the glass while signaling for a break.

"For all of you people who cling to your all-American values, which amount to a myopic nation lacking diversity and character, I say that the day you return the checks you get from unemployment, the overtime pay you earn after forty hours, and the Social Security checks you get upon retirement, then and only then will I take your conservative rhetoric seriously. Until then, why don't you shut the hell up!"

While Mitch and Paul clash on traditional radio, a tall, slim host named Tony Stravell is ready to lead the nation's top podcast, *The Gray Forum*.

Recognized for his distinctive style of wearing sports blazers, baseball caps, and sneakers, he doesn't shy away from confronting the political establishment and addressing controversial topics with insight and honesty.

With his eyes fixed on Rob, his producer, Tony leans in and pulls the microphone closer to his mouth.

"Ladies and gentlemen, my name is Tony Stravell, and I'm the voice of the number one podcast in the nation, *The Gray Forum*. Unfiltered, unrestricted, and uncompromising, this platform leaves nothing out as we examine today's issues and hold accountable those seeking power, those in power, and those who refuse to relinquish it. Gaining true knowledge requires looking deep beyond the surface to uncover critical information. It's a way of thinking that questions the political establishment, challenges the corporate structure, and empowers the people."

Ruffling through his notes, Tony pauses his monologue to reflect on his childhood.

"As a kid, I remember my mother and I leaving church one Sunday. Just before we walked out the door, I noticed strobes flashing from a security alarm mounted on the wall. Curious, I watched the flickering lights as we headed to our car. I kept reflecting on the pastor's sermon about God's protection. Once I got into the back seat, I reached forward, tapped my mother on the shoulder, and asked, 'Mom, if God protects us as the pastor said, then why do churches have alarms?'"

Tony looks at Rob as he recalls the experience.

"Stunned by the question, my mother turned around and looked at me as if I had said something wrong. From her expression, I could tell she was trying to find an answer to what I thought was a simple question. Confused, she turned back around, fastened her seat belt, and started the car. She never answered the question as the ride home grew unusually quiet. However, that marked the beginning of a mindset that shaped me into the curious person I am today."

Realizing he had gone off topic, Tony glances at Rob and refocuses on his thoughts.

"For decades, we have been misinformed, misled, deceived, and betrayed by a two-party system that pretends to be oppositional yet meets in private to craft public policy. What happened to legislative policies created by the people and for the people? What happened to proposals that would lower the cost of living so that the average family can afford basic amenities? How about someone devising a realistic plan to provide affordable housing for everyone, especially our veterans? Most disgraceful is our failure to develop a blueprint that allows people to access affordable health care without forcing families to drain their savings or file for bankruptcy to cover the costs."

Tony shakes his head in disappointment.

"Let me clarify this: I support the principles of capitalism and am completely against living in a socialist society; however, if our free-market system focuses only on maximizing profits and satisfying shareholders while ignoring the daily struggles faced by the people of this nation, then we'll continue to be in trouble!"

Tony, agitated by the topic, lowers his voice and regains his composure.

"Listen, I said it before, and I'll say it again. The problem is that too many Americans are distracted and unknowingly adopt a term I coined: top-layer politics. Some of you who are new to my program might ask, 'What are top-layer politics?' This is the spread of political talking points meant to skim the surface of the water like oil, hiding everything beneath. Top-layer politics are intended to obscure the real threats lurking below and direct our focus only on the superficial. I believe the devil is in the details, and the truth lies deep beneath the surface."

Rob raises his hand and signals for a break as Tony wraps up his opening monologue.

"This is Tony Stravell on *The Gray Forum*. Please support my podcast and remember: What you see on the surface is meant for you to see. We'll be right back after a word from our sponsors."

2

The Aftershow

The time nears six o'clock as Mitch stands at his desk, wrapping up his show.

"Ladies and gentlemen, you've heard from the best, and now you'll have to listen to the rest. I'm out!"

Mitch pushes his chair out of the way and heads to the elevator before getting into his car. As he drives through the busy streets of Manhattan, he arrives at the All-American Tavern to meet a friend. When he enters the bar, everyone waves and greets him with shouts of excitement:

"Mitch!"

Mitch smiles and nods as he takes a seat at the bar. His friend John arrives a few minutes later, sits next to Mitch, and pats him on the back.

"What's up, Mitch? How's it going?"

Mitch looks at John.

"Everything is good. What about you?"

"I'm good."

John signals for the bartender.

"Hey, do you want a drink?"

Mitch looks at him with a puzzled look on his face.

"Now, you know I don't drink alcohol."

John laughs and replies.

"Just checking. I'm not sure if I should trust a man who doesn't drink. It's like trying to trust a skinny chef . . . It's hard because you know he's not eating the food."

John chuckles at his own remarks while Mitch looks at him, shakes his head, and turns to the bartender.

"Let me have a virgin mojito, light on the ice."

John looks at Mitch, laughs, and then says, "Yeah, let me have the same thing, but leave out the mojito and the ice!"

Mitch looks at John, shakes his head, and replies, "Still the same John."

John laughs and looks at Mitch.

"Still the same faithful Mitch."

While Mitch and John talk at the bar, a group of young men playing pool notice Mitch from across the room. Suddenly, they change their conversation from sports to discussing Mitch's talk show.

The debate among them becomes so intense that when Mitch hears his name echoing repeatedly, he walks to the back of the room.

John reaches out to stop him, but it's already too late. Mitch is already staring at everyone as he approaches the pool table.

"It's apparent that you guys have a problem with me."

A young African American man, dressed in business casual attire, including a baseball cap and khaki pants, steps away from the group to approach Mitch.

"Yeah, that's right. We do."

Mitch looks at the young man.

"What's wrong? You can't handle the truth?"

The young man sizes up Mitch. "You look like you played football. Tell me, how can the playing field for African Americans be fair if one team starts every game at the fifty-yard line and the other farther back at the twenty? Either the team with the advantage would have to be held back, or the team with the disadvantage would have to be pushed forward. But there's one undeniable truth: If the rules stay the same, the situation will not change."

Curiosity and grumbles fill the tavern, and the crowd converges as Mitch responds to a young man half his age and size.

"If seventy percent of the players on the football field are African Americans, how can they have a disadvantage? Even more, how are these millionaires, playing a child's game, still being discriminated against today? Hell, the players even have their own national anthem played at the games. To me, that sounds like a nation working hard to accommodate an injustice!"

The young man looks at Mitch in amazement.

"Really? . . . So, you think an anthem that is meant to give hope, dignity, and recognition to African Americans is a solution to years of oppression? What about the long-term effects of oppression? How do we catch up, or better yet, what about reparations?"

Mitch looks at the young man, perplexed.

"Reparations? Are you serious? I believe those who experienced slavery and oppression should be considered, but a young man like you, who has everything to gain in today's digital society, deserves nothing. Your generation is blessed to live in a nation and era where technology and education can level the playing field, not reparations!"

The atmosphere and tone in the tavern shift dramatically. John, watching from the bar, grows increasingly concerned while observing the discussion. He has known Mitch for years and is aware of Mitch's temper.

Now, the young man is triggered. He walks up to Mitch and stands inches away from his large frame.

"You don't have to go back to slavery to see the lasting damage of oppression. Not long ago, a famous comedian told a worldwide audience that because of racism, his mother, as a young girl, was not legally allowed to go to a White dentist. Instead, she had to humiliate herself and find an animal doctor to pull her tooth. That did not happen four hundred years ago; this was during your lifetime!"

The young man continues speaking passionately, pointing his finger at Mitch's face.

"How do you think that inhumane experience affected her? What else was she legally denied from childhood to adulthood? And if I don't deserve reparations, what about someone like her, who was not enslaved but faced blatant racism?"

Irritated, Mitch gently pushes the young man's finger away from his face.

"I don't believe that money can fix the wrongs of the past. Nor can the mental and spiritual harm inflicted on African Americans because of past injustices be fixed through government action."

The young man listens carefully as Mitch continues.

"My family was not part of the unjust system that enslaved your ancestors. In fact, my grandparents were immigrants to this country. They barely survived the bombings of war. My father and his sister were moved from one bombed-out building to another to avoid death. They often ate scraps left by those who had fled their homes and sometimes had to drink water dripping from leaking pipes. Like you, we are also victims of man's inhumanity to man. So, why should we have to pay for the sins of others?"

Frustrated, the young man glares at Mitch.

"I understand your point, but you failed to answer my question."

Again, the young man points his finger in Mitch's face.

"Does the woman who was denied dental care deserve . . ."

But before he can finish, Mitch abruptly slaps the young man's hand away with enough force that the sound echoes throughout the bar. Then he shouts:

"Don't you ever point your finger at me again!"

The young man withdraws his hand but shows no fear in response to Mitch's aggression. Despite the hit, he keeps eye contact with Mitch, determined not to back down. John, hearing the noise, rushes to the back of the bar and joins the young man's friends to separate the two and calm things down.

Once apart, the young man composes himself, looks at his friends, and nods. Mitch, noticing movement out of the corner of his eye, tries to keep his focus on both the young man and his friends at the same time. Suddenly, Mitch and John find themselves surrounded by five of the young man's friends.

The bar's atmosphere shifts as the crowd realizes that something is about to go down. People step back, leaving only Mitch, John, the young man, and his friends standing together.

In defiance, the young man speaks.

"Now, what do you want to do? According to your law, I have the right to defend myself from a right-wing nutcase whose arrogance led him to believe he could hit me and get away with it!"

Surrounded, Mitch stares at the young man and says nothing as he continues his rant.

"You know what, Mr. Talk Show? I'm a God-fearing man, just like you. You're blessed because, after you put your hands on me, things could have gotten ugly. But because . . ."

At that moment, the bartender, carrying a shotgun, approaches the young man and his friends.

"All right, enough is enough! This is my place, and I'm not looking for any trouble. So, you guys need to leave!"

Confused, the young man looks at the bartender.

"Wait! This man approached my friends and me while we were talking and playing pool, disrupted our conversation, tried to intimidate me, and then hit me. Yet you're throwing us out?"

An awkward silence falls over the room. The young man stares at the bartender, who says nothing. Frustrated, the young man turns to his friends.

"Come on, guys, let's get out of here!"

In a New York second, they grab their stuff, drop their pool sticks, and leave the bar.

Outside, the young man glances back at the sign on the building and pulls one of his friends aside.

"David, you came here to play pool, but look at the sign on the building. I didn't notice it when we walked in, but what does it say?"

David looks up.

"It says, 'All-American Tavern.'"

The young man looks at him.

"Why do you think the word *all* is there? The sign doesn't say 'American Tavern' or 'National Tavern.' It says, 'All-American Tavern.' Do you know what that means?"

David looks up at the sign.

"No."

"Don't you know your history? It means that your Black ass is not welcome there!"

David says, "Is that right?

"Yeah, that's right!"

David curiously looks at him.

"But until we had a beef with that talk show guy, we were having a good time. Nobody bothered us, and we were chillin'. I don't get it!"

The young man sighs in frustration and pats David on the back.

"That's the problem, my brother. You don't get it!"
"Let's get out of here! I have projects to complete."

While a frustrated, embarrassed, and somewhat remorseful Mitch talks to John about the confrontation with the young man, Paul wraps up his show for the night.

"Living in today's high-tech society offers significant advantages, particularly for the underprivileged. I believe technology has the potential to reduce the disparity between the haves and the have-nots and close the prosperity gap. However, to achieve this, we need to build a strong foundation for our educational system. Giving a child a computer isn't enough if they can't read at grade level. It's also unrealistic to expect a child to learn when they're hungry or in need of food. For those of you who are Christians, remember that your Bible states, 'For when I was hungry, you gave me food, and when I was thirsty, you gave me a drink.'"

Paul raises his voice as he speaks into the microphone.

"What happened to the political party that once called itself the party of family values? How can cutting funding for school meal programs be seen as helping families? Why is reducing the budget for essential needs like food, shelter, and education considered a good move? The great nation of Rome was eventually destroyed from within, and if we continue on a path that ignores the welfare of its own citizens, we risk a similar collapse. Have a good evening!"

Paul, feeling mentally exhausted, waves to Rochelle, grabs his bag, and heads to his car. Before going to the garage, he decides to stop at a local coffee shop across the street. As he walks toward the shop, he notices two men hanging out in the doorway. Always alert, Paul cautiously approaches the entrance, knowing that encountering loiterers is sometimes part of city life. However, situations can change suddenly.

When Paul reaches the coffee shop, one guy is on the right side of the door, rolling a joint, while another is on the left, smoking one. People enter and leave the coffee shop, ignoring the guys, but for some reason, when Paul reaches for the door, the guy on the left blows marijuana smoke into his face.

Whether the guy did it on purpose doesn't matter; Paul isn't having it. He is not a fighter, but he is a New Yorker and not one to back down from a confrontation. He looks the guy straight in the eye.

"Really, what is your problem?"

The guy looks at Paul as if he is not doing anything wrong.

"You just blew smoke in my face!"

The guy smirks and offers no apology. With a line forming behind him at the door, Paul stares at the guy, saying nothing. Finally, he turns, looks behind him at the people waiting, and goes inside to get a cup of coffee.

While waiting in line, he overheard the young man at the door talking loudly to his friend outside.

"Man, I should have punched that guy in the face. Who the hell does he think he is?"

His friend nods in agreement, and the young man continues.

"Yeah, you saw me. I stood strong, looked him dead in the eyes, and he walked away!"

Irritated, Paul gets out of line, walks outside, and points at the guy.

"Let me explain something to you. If it weren't for people like me, you wouldn't be able to stand out here and smoke weed without the fear of getting arrested. The legalization of weed was meant for personal and private use, not for punks like you who are standing on the street, invading other people's personal space with your smoke!"

With that, Paul forgets about his coffee and heads to his car. Stunned, one of the guys turns to the other.

"Who the hell was he?"

His friend appears confused and says, "I don't know."

As Paul leaves, a middle-aged man wearing a baseball cap overhears the conversation. He addresses the young men in a firm yet calm tone.

"Hey, just want to let you know that the man who spoke to you is Paul Vorbont, a key voice in the legalization of marijuana in our city. He stops by here occasionally for coffee and deserves respect, so please, don't disrespect him."

The guys glance at each other and laugh.

"Listen, I'm serious! If you mess with him and marijuana laws aren't renewed next year, you'll be seeing me again, and I promise you, it won't be pretty!"

With that quick statement and a stare that means business, the man walks away. Stunned, the guys look at each other.

"Can you believe this? We're getting threatened just for enjoying a little weed. I don't care about that guy, Paul, or that fool who tried to intimidate us. To hell with them!"

They laugh and move farther from the entrance, continuing to smoke their weed.

Meanwhile, while driving home, Paul feels troubled by the earlier confrontation and questions whether he should have supported stricter marijuana regulations.

At *The Gray Forum*, Tony continues to excel with the nation's top podcast. He discusses a range of topics, emphasizing the interconnectedness within the country's two-party system.

"The truth is that when fewer people vote, those in power have a better chance of maintaining their positions. While they may claim to promote voting, they often prefer that you stay home. This is especially true in local elections, where the outcome can turn on just a few hundred or a few thousand votes. Sadly, this contradictory behavior is seen in both political parties, which is why this platform exists."

Tony drinks some water as he continues.

"My goal is to uncover hidden information, bring it to light, and share it with everyone. To make my efforts effective, I need an audience that is willing to think critically, unafraid to explore the unknown, and open to new theories and ideas."

Tony gets excited as he continues.

"That is why my broadcast airs when the average commuter can listen, from five to eight p.m. I capture the typical person leaving work and stay with them until they arrive home. I take more callers on my show than any other talk show nationwide. I refuse to make you wait on hold for forty-five minutes just to be rushed off after thirty seconds of speaking. I respect your time. I want to hear from you. I need to know what's happening in your life. My emphasis on your personal experience offers a more complete picture, socially and economically, than any information from the big corporate-owned radio stations across the country."

At 7:58 p.m., Rob gestures for Tony to conclude the show. With enthusiasm, Tony gathers his belongings and wraps up the podcast.

"Family, please remember that this show wouldn't be possible without you and your support, and always keep in mind: What you see on the surface is meant for you to see. Have a great night."

As Tony packs his things, Rob looks at him.

"Hey, Tony, what are you doing tonight?"

Tony looks at Rob.

"Usually, I would go over to Nicole's house for dinner, but her spoiled son really bothers me. Don't get me wrong; he isn't disrespectful, but he has a crazy sense of entitlement, especially when it comes to working. Even worse, if I try to tell him about the importance of being persistent and relentless in pursuing his goals, he looks at me like I'm crazy. Then Nicole gets upset with me for upsetting her son!"

Rob listens intently as Tony continues to share his feelings.

"Maybe it's just me. I have worked so hard to reach this point in my life that I cannot understand the lack of hustle and carefree attitude this generation has toward work."

Rob sympathizes.

"I hear you, Tony. It's a tough situation. I know you only want the best for Nicole and her son."

Tony nods his head and walks toward the door.

"Listen, I appreciate you and your words. Have a good night."

3

Family Ties

Night falls as Mitch pulls into his complex in Long Island. He approaches the guard's booth, exchanges a subtle nod with the security staff, and passes through the massive iron gate. He drives along a softly lit road and turns right onto a winding, wooded path that leads to a castle-like residence.

Mitch parks his car in the cobblestone driveway and sits silently, lost in thought, for a few minutes. Still irritated by his encounter with the young man, he walks toward the front door. His wife, Jean, greets him. She reaches out to embrace Mitch and welcomes him as he returns her hug with little enthusiasm.

"Hey, honey, how was your day?"

Looking aggravated, Mitch responds, "Okay."

"That's it? Just okay?"

Mitch snaps back. "That's what I said."

Ironically, this is not the first time Mitch has returned home frustrated after his talk show appearance. As his political influence grew, so did his recognition, and as his popularity increased, demand for his time also rose. His success places enormous pressure on him to lead the conservative cause. However, the demands on his time take a toll on his marriage, leaving Mitch with little time left to nurture the relationship.

As Jean heads into the kitchen to prepare dinner, Mitch walks into the living room, sits on the couch, and stares at the television, which has no picture. His ego can't help but constantly recall the events at the bar, wondering what he could have said or done to challenge the young man's argument.

Jean senses that something beyond Mitch's typical day has happened, but decides not to say anything. She believes in living a life centered on being a supportive wife. So, whenever Mitch comes home in one of his moods, she tries to exercise patience, giving him time to unwind.

Before becoming pregnant and a stay-at-home mom, Jean had a distinguished career as a model, appearing in artistic photo shoots for magazines, clothing displays, and commercial print campaigns. She met Mitch twenty-five years ago while working on a campaign for his radio station. Now that her two daughters are in college, she is feeling restless and wants to explore new opportunities in her field.

Jean eventually brings Mitch his dinner, hoping that a good meal will help him relax.

"Mitch, you seem like you have a lot on your mind, but we need to talk."

Mitch rolls his eyes and says nothing while eating his dinner.

"I want to work and earn some money while I still can. Many reputable modeling agencies still need women like me to work for them. I don't understand your problem with me going to work."

Mitch looks up at Jean while speaking with a mouthful of food.

"I don't have a problem. I have concerns."

Jean places her hands on her hips and glares at Mitch. "Maybe I'm overlooking something. Are you certain your hesitation isn't a way to exert control? After all, they say people who grew up as an only child are accustomed to controlling things."

Mitch inquisitively looks up at Jean as she continues making her point.

"In fact, you had this controlling streak even when we were dating."

Mitch continues to stare at Jean. "What are you talking about?"

Jean rolls her eyes.

"Remember, three months into dating, I needed a massage, and we had a serious argument because you said no."

Mitch starts to think back. "How do you remember these things? I vaguely recall you wanting a massage and me disagreeing. It was so long ago."

Mitch stops eating and tries to recall as Jean stands over him with her hands folded.

"Hold on! Yes, I remember! That turned into a big argument. You usually had a masseuse named Gale give you a massage, but she wasn't available, so you were willing to let George give you one. That's where I had an issue."

Jean stares at Mitch as if he is making her point.

"There shouldn't have been an issue! It was my choice. This is where your controlling mindset leads to problems."

Mitch looks at Jean, recalling how he felt at that moment.

"Listen, when we were dating, you told me your body was off-limits until there was a solid commitment, and I accepted that. However, later, when your body was aching, and Gale was unavailable, you were planning to let Big George touch you all over. Now, how does that sound? Big George gets to see you naked and feel you all over without a commitment, while I have to wine, dine, plead, and pray to win your affection!"

Jean waves her hand at Mitch, dismissing his claims as he keeps talking.

"To make things worse, this guy George gets a free ride because you're paying him to touch you. Heck, I would have done it for free!"

Jean tries to follow up with an answer, but Mitch cuts her off.

"Listen, I don't want to talk about this anymore because it's getting me pissed off again. To answer your question, I was being rational, not controlling!"

Jean stands in front of Mitch, and he ignores her as he keeps eating. He knows one thing she cannot tolerate is being ignored. It's an emotional trigger that takes her back to her childhood. Still, he does it anyway, and now, she is furious.

"Mitch, look at me. Don't ignore me! What the hell is wrong with me going back to work?"

Mitch, taken aback by her tone, set his fork down and responds sarcastically. "Wow, what happened to your Christian values?"

Jean replies, "They went out the window when you minimized my feelings. You purposely drove me to this point!"

Mitch places his plate down on the coffee table.

"Hey, you're a grown woman. I can't make you do anything; take some responsibility."

Jean snaps back, "I'm trying to take responsibility, but you have a problem with me making decisions that I believe are best for me!"

Knowing he wants no drama all night, Mitch looks up. "All right, Jean, I'm listening. How do you know there are any opportunities in the industry for a model housewife in her late forties?"

Jean looks at her husband with an optimistic sneer, as if she's finally gotten his attention.

"I researched social media. There are many opportunities for a woman in my situation to reenter the modeling industry. It's a new world out there, with technology that can boost my strengths and reduce my weaknesses, even at my age."

Mitch rubs his forehead in frustration and looks at his wife.

"Look, I told you before, you can't believe everything on the internet, especially social media. To make matters worse, with the rise of artificial intelligence, everything online seems authentic and legitimate. In my view, the internet has become a cesspool of deception."

Jean sighs and rolls her eyes as Mitch raises his voice and keeps talking.

"Sometimes it feels like I'm going in circles with this. As I've mentioned before, my duty is to provide for and protect you. I cannot fulfill that responsibility if we're commuting to Manhattan separately every day. What if someone recognizes you and discovers I'm your husband? They could confront or threaten you because of my beliefs and my show. That's a risk I'm not willing to take!"

Jean looks at Mitch in disbelief.

"Maybe you're hesitant to take the risk, but I'm not. Are you saying that I can't handle myself?"

Mitch smirks and frowns at Jean in frustration.

"Did you hear what I just said? It's my job to care for you and this family! My success in broadcasting brings blessings and stability to this household. But my voice can also cause resentment and anger in others. Don't you want a husband who is preventative and proactive about your safety?"

Jean scowls at Mitch. She's had enough of his condescending, fatherly tone, so she walks out of the room. However, it isn't long before she storms back in and stands in front of him with both hands on her hips.

"Do you believe God is powerful enough to care for me?"

Mitch stops eating and looks at Jean, shocked by the question she just asked.

"Excuse me?"

"Do you believe our God is powerful enough to care for me?"

Mitch looks at Jean with curiosity, wondering where she's headed.

"Yes."

Jean turns her back on Mitch and begins walking toward the kitchen.

"Really . . . as a so-called man of faith, it seems like you lack faith!"

Mitch, now furious, watches Jean walk away and yells, "You know, Jean, to hell with it! If you want to go to Manhattan, go ahead! Just don't ask me anything!"

Jean shouts back from the kitchen, "Wow, what happened to your Christian values?"

Mitch is now fuming. He walks toward the kitchen, just loud enough for Jean to hear him. "Listen, I can't be a man only when it suits you, then try to turn off my manhood when you want your way. This light doesn't just switch on and off. I am who I am, and that's a man!"

Silence fills the air as Mitch turns around and goes back to the living room. As if he didn't already have enough on his mind, Jean's words spark something inside Mitch.

With an uneasy quietness filling the living room, aside from the faint clang of dishes from the kitchen, Mitch thinks about the young man at the tavern, then about Jean's words. After some reflection, he looks around his home, shakes his head, and mutters to himself.

"Wow! After all these years and everything I've done for her, she still doesn't respect me."

In frustration, he throws his plate onto the coffee table, spilling food on the floor, and then heads upstairs for the night.

Paul also has had his share of reflecting on his day. Paul's peaceful trip home is overshadowed by the tension from his earlier confrontation with the hoodlums at the bodega. As he pulls into the dimly lit garage of his co-op on the Upper East Side, he rummages through the clutter in his armrest to find his key card. His fingers finally tap against the small plastic card. With a sigh of relief, he places it in front of the reader, and the gate slowly lifts open while he steers the car inside.

Paul has always held liberal views. Although he is not religious, he believes everyone should be treated with dignity and respect. He struggles with those who share his views but take liberal ideology to an extreme, infuriating moderates within the Democratic Party.

As Paul parks his car in his designated spot, he grabs his bags, clicks the alarm on his BMW, and heads toward the elevator. After a long day, his ride in the elevator feels like an endless tunnel as he reflects on how frustrating it is to deal with politicians who lack commitment. As the elevator stops on the seventeenth floor, he slowly makes his way to his apartment.

Just as he inserts his key card into the door, it swings open. His wife is there to greet him. "Honey, so glad you're home. How was your day?"

Paul looks aggravated and tired as he hugs his wife.

"Kelly, I feel like a voice crying out in the city, and nobody hears me."

Paul's wife is accustomed to his disheartened mindset after a long day. He has been broadcasting for over twenty years and has built a loyal following for his cause. His respect within the liberal and Democratic parties is impressive; however, even with his influence and voice, he cannot overcome the power of corporate interests.

Kelly looks at Paul with compassion as she gently touches his face.

"Come, sweetheart, and relax. Your dinner is almost ready, and the boys are in their rooms."

Paul walks past the living room and toward his office. He sets his bag on his desk and heads down the hall to the boys' rooms. They're teenagers, and Paul encourages them to think critically, fostering their own mindsets. He has always maintained a close and open relationship with his sons. They've done well in school and always looked forward to their father coming home—until now.

As Paul approaches his son Preston's door and knocks, he waits a few seconds but gets no reply. When he opens it, he sees his son isn't in the room and mutters to himself.

"He's probably with his brother in his room."

Paul takes a short walk down the hall to his son Pierce's room. He knocks on the closed door, eager to see him, but after a few moments of silence, he receives no response. Growing a bit concerned, Paul heads to the kitchen, where his wife is cooking.

"Kelly, where are the boys?"

Kelly looks at Paul while placing the dinner plates on the table.

"I don't know. If they're not in their rooms, they might be on the balcony. That's probably why they can't hear you."

Paul smiles and nods in agreement as he walks toward the balcony. There's nothing like the view of the sunset in the city. It's the main reason Paul and his family have stayed in their apartment while others moved to the suburbs.

Paul's parents moved into the building decades ago when it was just a rent-stabilized three-bedroom apartment. However, when the owners sold the building, the new owners converted it into a cooperative. As longtime residents, Paul's parents received free shares in their unit to encourage them to stay. When the opportunity arose, Paul's parents decided to move to Florida, leaving the apartment to Paul. They return to New York City every year for Christmas because there's no better place to celebrate the holiday.

Still searching for his sons, Paul walks through the living room to the curtains covering a floor-to-ceiling window. With anticipation, he reaches for the handle to open the balcony door, only to find it locked. Curious, he steps back, examines the handle, and tries to open it again. Once more, the door refuses to budge. Frustrated, Paul begins knocking on the balcony door.

"Preston and Pierce, are you out there?"

As he stands at the door, he can barely hear movement coming from the balcony.

"Preston and Pierce, I know you're out there . . . Open this door!"

Slowly, the door to the balcony opens just enough for Preston to show his face and respond to his father.

"We're out here, Dad. What's the problem?"

Preston stands in the doorway, blocking Paul's ability to enter the balcony.

"Why is this door locked, and what are you and your brother doing?"

Preston, looking tense, responds, "Dad, we're just chillin."

Paul now has a suspicious look on his face as he sticks his head through the balcony door and looks around.

"Son, move out of the way so I can talk to you and your brother!"

Preston pauses and looks at his brother, who shrugs his shoulders and slowly steps aside. Paul enters and glances around the screened-in balcony, its length lined with chairs and a gas grill.

Walking along, he heads to the far end of the balcony and spots his son, Pierce, relaxing in a lawn chair. Pierce sits up when his father approaches.

"What's up, Dad?"

Paul looks around curiously, sensing that something is wrong. Usually, at this time of the evening, his sons would be in their rooms playing video games. They have never relished or appreciated the sunset the way he does.

As Paul stands at the balcony's edge, taking in the view, a light breeze blows, and the smell of marijuana drifts from the back of the balcony. Clearly irritated, Paul begins inspecting himself and sniffing his shirt, thinking the smoke residue might have come from the coffee shop encounter. But when the weed smell grows stronger, Paul's expression shifts, and he looks back at Pierce.

"Hey! Are you guys smoking weed out here?"

Pierce responds, "What are you talking about, Dad?"

"You know what I'm talking about!"

Paul looks around the balcony. "Pierce, get your ass out of that chair . . . Get up!"

As Pierce stands up from the chair, Paul grabs it and throws it to the other side of the balcony, almost hitting the grill. There, lying on the floor in the corner of the balcony, is a still-lit, half-smoked, rolled-up joint.

Paul's eyes widen as he looks at Pierce.

"What the hell is this?"

Preston walks over, examines the joint on the floor, then looks at Paul, stunned.

"Dad, I had no idea."

Then Preston points at Pierce.

"Pierce, I'm surprised at you!"

Paul skeptically looks at Preston.

"Shut up, Preston!" Pierce says.

Paul walks to the balcony door and shouts, "Kelly! Kelly! . . . Can you come here, please?"

Kelly is down the hall, but she can hear Paul shouting her name.

"Coming . . ."

As she turns off the stove, she rushes down the hall to see what Paul is yelling about. Paul is standing in the doorway, keeping the boys on the balcony as if they were prisoners.

"Kelly, you're not going to believe what your boys were doing on the balcony." Paul points his finger at Preston and Pierce. "These knuckleheads were smoking weed!"

Kelly looks up with a sigh of relief. Paul is visibly confused.

"I said your boys were smoking weed on my balcony!"

Kelly, visibly frustrated, looks to Paul with a glare. "I heard you the first time. I'm disappointed in the boys."

Kelly moves Paul aside from the doorway, steps onto the balcony, and approaches the boys.

"Boys, whether it's cigarettes or weed, we don't allow any smoking in our home. Do you understand?"

The boys nod their heads and respond simultaneously, "Yes, ma'am."

Then Kelly walks off the balcony, slides past Paul, and heads toward the kitchen.

Paul is stunned by her response. He closes the balcony door, leaving the boys outside, and follows his wife into the kitchen.

"What was that?" he demands.

Kelly looks baffled as she finishes dinner.

"What do you mean?"

Paul raises his voice. "Your response regarding the boys smoking weed did not include any punishment!"

Kelly places some pots in the sink and looks at Paul. "Would you rather they smoke on the balcony or in the streets?"

Stunned, Paul says, "Kelly, Preston is sixteen, and Pierce is fifteen. I would rather they not smoke at all!"

Kelly looks at Paul and smiles. "Well, you're the one who lobbied for weed to be legal in New York."

Paul is baffled as to why Kelly is bringing this up.

"You're right. However, there are age restrictions. Our boys are not old enough or mature enough to handle the adverse effects weed can have on the mind and body."

Kelly places another pot in the sink.

"Then why did you lobby for its legalization? Pierce and Preston know you're in favor of marijuana use, and now you're punishing them for something you support?"

A frustrated Paul can't believe what he's hearing.

"Really, Kelly? You have worked in education and with teens for over twenty years before retiring. You know the damage weed can do to young people. What I'm saying isn't hypocritical, just sensible. I don't believe anyone should be locked up or acquire a criminal record for buying and smoking weed. Most people want the government to stay out of their personal affairs, so this is an example where the government should mind its own business. It just makes sense!"

Paul storms out of the kitchen, heads to the balcony, opens the door, and approaches his sons.

"All right, boys, you're grounded from all activities until you're of legal age to smoke!"

Preston looks confused. "How long is that?"

Paul looks at them with a skeptical expression.

"You smoke weed and don't know? Go to your rooms and figure it out!"

As his sons leave, Paul goes to the balcony and cleans up the mess they left behind. When he finishes, he closes the door and hears Pierce shout, "Twenty-one? Oh no!"

Paul smirks while heading to the kitchen for dinner.

Meanwhile, Tony is in his car, looking forward to dining at a new cosmopolitan restaurant in Harlem.

As far as he is concerned, Harlem remains the cultural and diverse heart of New York City. Its history serves as a road map, highlighting the community's struggles and resilience.

Tony was a young African American boy raised in Harlem, who was curious from an early age and always marched to the beat of his own drum. As a kid, he would ask his parents thought-provoking questions about dinosaurs and when God created them. As he grew older, he began to challenge the status quo, questioning anyone or anything that sought to limit his potential. Tony developed a wait-and-see approach to life and his personal beliefs. Despite his parents' religious convictions, he came to the logical conclusion that there was no definitive proof for or against the existence of God.

Twenty minutes later, Tony turns the corner and finds a parking spot two blocks from the Harmony Soul House. It is an upscale five-star restaurant specializing in Southern and Caribbean cuisine. Tony has made a reservation for 9:00 p.m. and is standing in the restaurant's vestibule, waiting for his girlfriend to arrive. He looks into the dining room and notices a dimly lit yet charming atmosphere, filled with the sultry sounds of smooth jazz. It is just what he needs after a long day.

Five minutes later, a smiling Nicole arrives and hugs Tony. "Good to see you."

Tony looks Nicole up and down and smiles at her. "It's good to be seen. You look great!"

Nicole smiles. "Oh, thank you!"

As they move from the vestibule to the dining room, the host greets them, scrolls through a touch-screen tablet, and confirms their reservation.

"Good evening, Mr. Stravell, and thank you for dining at the Harmony Soul House. Please follow me."

They approach a table positioned in the center of the floor, offering a fantastic view of the band. The background music creates a smooth, melodic atmosphere that echoes throughout the restaurant. It's loud enough to feel the vibe but low enough to allow for conversation. It is the perfect setting for a date.

Nicole has been looking forward to this night. She met Tony as a caller on his podcast. She works in finance but has always been somewhat of an advocate for those who cannot help themselves.

One evening, while browsing social media, she saw the headline, "Aren't You Tired of the Same Old Political Crap?" Intrigued, she knew it was clickbait but still tuned in to hear what Tony had to say. Later, she gathered the courage to call in to the show, and it didn't take long for Tony to become captivated by her intelligence and convictions. Soon after, Tony started chatting with Nicole off the air, and seven years later, they are still a committed couple.

About ten minutes after they've been praising the decor and atmosphere, a manager approaches and whispers to Tony and Nicole, "Good evening. I apologize for the inconvenience. The host misassigned your seating; this table is reserved for out-of-town visitors only. Allow me to show you another table that is just as comfortable."

Tony stares at the manager in disbelief. "Excuse me?"

The manager responds in his smooth, articulate voice. "Here at the Harmony Soul House, we strive to serve out-of-town visitors so they can experience the flavor and essence of Southern and Caribbean cuisine."

Tony is stunned, and his eyes widen as he looks at the manager.

"I booked my reservation well in advance, and as a Harlem resident, why should I give up my seat to out-of-towners who may not appreciate the food and atmosphere you've created here?"

The manager, with a hint of concern in his voice, continues to plead his request, as if he hasn't heard anything Tony has said.

"Yes, sir, I'm saying that we try to cater to out-of-towners so they can experience our dining menu while on vacation. I kindly ask you to relocate your seat."

Things get tense as the host brings over a couple visiting from Missouri to Tony's table. Now the manager, the waiter, and the couple are standing around Tony and Nicole, waiting for them to move.

After an uncomfortable minute, Tony stands and says to the manager in a stern, calm voice, "Am I being pranked? This is unbelievable. I'm in the community and of the community. I'm not moving!"

Now, the other customers become agitated as the band continues to play. Those seated in the middle of the restaurant are now complaining to waitstaff, not because Tony and Nicole are being unfairly treated, but because their view of the band is blocked.

However, the murmuring of customers around Tony does not bother him. Worried that things might worsen, the manager glances around at the diners, then turns to Tony.

"Please, sir, I understand your frustration; however, I'm kindly asking you to move to another table."

Worried that the situation is spiraling out of control, Nicole grabs Tony's arm, pulls him down to his seat, and whispers in his ear. "Please, Tony, let's just move."

Tony can barely hold back his anger. He stands up again, looks at the manager, then turns to his left and sees the host and the couple patiently waiting. Then he turns to his right and sees customers visibly agitated by the distraction.

"All right, all right, we'll move. Come on, Nicole, let's go."

Just as Tony and Nicole stand up, the out-of-town couple takes their seats. As Tony grabs his coat from the chair, the visiting gentleman looks at him and says with a halfhearted smile, "Sorry about that."

Then he looks at his wife, smiles, and sits down.

In the midst of the chaos, the manager approaches Tony, looking relieved.

"Thank you, sir. Please follow me. Right this way."

The manager leads Tony and Nicole to a different table, three sections over to the right from their original seat. As Nicole sits down, the manager addresses Tony.

"Sir, thank you for cooperating. I know it was an inconvenience. Please, let me take care of your drinks and appetizers."

Tony, frustrated, moves closer to the manager to avoid making a scene.

"Listen, I don't need you to pay for our drinks or appetizers. I can cover them myself. You embarrassed me in front of everyone, especially my lady. So, let me ask you: Where do I go, and what can you offer me to get my respect back?"

There is a pause as the manager, gazing at Tony with an apologetic look, turns and walks away. Tony watches him until he is out of sight. Then he sits down and focuses on Nicole.

"Sweetheart, I'm sorry about all of this. If I had stood my ground and not moved, all hell would have broken loose. Everyone saw them seat us, and no one stood up to support us. Where is the community in that?"

Nicole attentively listens to Tony, noticing he is clearly annoyed.

"And to top it off, the manager offered to cover our drinks and appetizers to show he was sorry for the situation. We know it's just a gesture to keep us quiet, especially in an age where social media reviews can make or break a restaurant."

Then Tony looks at Nicole compassionately, takes her hand, and kisses it.

"Listen, the night is still young; let's get out of here and go somewhere else. You deserve better!"

Nicole nods in agreement as a waiter delivers two complimentary drinks from the manager. Tony and Nicole quietly get up and leave the restaurant.

Tony escorts Nicole to her car, then gets in himself. He glances at her, momentarily at a loss for words, as he reflects on the evening. While Nicole searches for another restaurant on her phone, Tony shakes his head in frustration, reaches for her hand, and gives it a gentle squeeze.

"Sweetheart, I usually don't talk about bad dining experiences on my podcast, but after what happened tonight, I must make an exception. Nobody's going to believe it!"

4

Commanding Act

At six two, slim, and clean-shaven with slicked-back brown hair, he is an obscure figure who seems to appear from nowhere. His political background is quite limited, and his rapid rise in the upcoming presidential race confuses many, especially his opponents. Despite this, Westyn Hale, an independent candidate, wins the primary election and secures a position in the national election by focusing on issues important to the working class. He has a strong talent for connecting with people, listening to their concerns, and reassuring them that better days are ahead.

Hale knows he faces a tough challenge against two major political parties backed by substantial funding. Still, he plans to raise campaign money by appealing to the people. Instead of spending heavily on traditional advertising, he decides to focus most of his budget on social media ads, which cost a tenth as much as conventional ads.

Hale recognizes that most people work hard all day, and by the time they return home, they are not interested in lengthy political policies. So, he intentionally focuses his platform on five key issues he believes will resonate with working folks.

One evening, as Hale and his associates leave a restaurant, a reporter approaches them with a microphone.

"Mr. Hale, you're new to politics, and honestly, I hadn't heard of you until you ran for president. However, you managed to attract a sizable portion of the population with your charismatic appeal. Besides your charm, what else do you bring to the table, and do you have genuine policies to support your campaign?"

Taken aback by the question and the boldness with which the reporter has addressed him, Hale pauses, looks him in the eyes, and says, "Sir, where have you been? I have spoken to the media throughout the primary elections, clearly outlining my policies. That's why I'm still in this race. But it's concerning that you ran up to me after dinner and talked as if you've never heard my platform."

Hale walks up to the reporter.

"So, let me make it straightforward for you. First, I want to lower taxes for the middle class and corporations as an incentive to foster a respectful fiscal relationship between the two. Without the working class, corporate visions are just ideas, and without corporate ingenuity, the idea of a viable middle class is nothing more than economic theory.

"Second, education should be accessible to everyone, not just the wealthy. When the NBA holds its draft, it gives the weakest team the best chance to pick a top player. Why?

Because they understand that strengthening weaker teams helps make the league stronger. Similarly, uplifting the underprivileged and poor helps to improve the nation as a whole.

"Third, how can anyone pursue their dreams if they're not in good health? We live in the greatest economy in the world, so why can't we have a basic government health care plan for everyone? I don't believe a country taking care of its people is socialism; it's protectionism. As the saying goes, 'A healthy nation is a strong nation.'

"Fourth, our military is the backbone of our democracy. Funding must be allocated to maintain the strength of our armed forces. New technology must be adopted to protect the nation. The stronger we are, the less vulnerable we become.

"Fifth, family values are fundamental to the social fabric of this great country. I believe in traditional family values; however, I also believe in the people's free will to make their own choices. Therefore, I won't judge others if they don't share my beliefs."

The reporter pauses to consider Hale's remarks. However, before asking another question, Hale interrupts.

"Did I answer your question about what I bring to the table?"

Still thinking, the reporter stares at Hale.

"Somewhat."

Hale smirks as he reaches out and shakes his hand.

"Well, that's it for me. Have a good night."

Just like that, the interview is over. Hale and his associates go to his car and drive away.

No one captures the spirit of political debate during an election year quite like New York City. The exchanges are raw and genuine, with listeners sharing their concerns and hopes for their candidates. As expected, each talk show host champions their party's stances as the race heads toward November.

"Welcome, you're listening to the one and only *Consultant of Conservatism* on WCONS in New York City. It's an election year, and I'm here to guide you on whom to vote for. You need my help to navigate through the media's confusion and filter out the facts so you can make an informed decision."

Mitch glances through the glass at Jake and smiles.

"Of course, because of my status and ratings as the top talk show host in the country, I have a lot of influence over who the next president will be. With over three hundred stations tuning in daily and tens of millions listening on the radio and online, my impact exceeds that of elected officials in Congress!"

Mitch adjusts his seat and continues.

"Did anyone read the interview with Westyn Hale after he left a restaurant last night? Who is this guy, and how did he slip through the primary election? Can you think of any other modern candidate who bases their platform on a Robin Hood political structure, essentially stealing from conservative policies to support their own agenda? This approach could be considered a political crime in other countries. In his political ignorance, Mr. Hale is trying to create a policy that pleases everyone. However, he overlooks the reality that it's impossible to satisfy everyone, especially in politics."

Mitch grabs his bottle and takes a drink of water.

"I give him credit for creating a platform that can be summarized into five key political points that are easy for the public to understand. However, the substance of his policies is not original; he has borrowed ideas on issues like tax cuts, military support, and family values from my party. While these concepts may sound appealing, they reveal the deceptive nature of his platform and campaign."

Mitch is visibly frustrated as he looks at Jake.

"Regardless of his fake candidacy, we're fortunate to have a Republican running for president who is a conservative. One who believes in Christian values and moral absolutism. One who supports pro-business principles rooted in capitalism as the economic foundation of this great nation."

Mitch runs his hand through his hair.

"I'm fed up with these weak-hearted politicians who sway easily. Please do not call my program to express your intention to vote for the Independent candidate. It's a wasted vote and a waste of time! I would rather you stay home than vote for any other candidate."

Mitch grabs the microphone from his desk.

"WCONS family, do me a favor, and listen to your Uncle Mitch. Vote Republican in November."

Jake signals that it's time for a break.

"This is Mitch Corvane. Stay right there. We'll be right back."

As the energy in New York City grows in anticipation of the upcoming election, the studio buzzes with excitement as Paul engages his audience with sharp insights, leaving no doubt about where he stands:

"Welcome back to WPROG in New York City! We're the top nationally syndicated liberal talk show in the country, and we're on the verge of one of the most critical elections of our lifetime. To make things even more interesting, we have an Independent candidate who has made it to the big dance. For those unfamiliar, that term refers to the teams that qualify for the NCAA college basketball tournament."

Paul takes a sip of his coffee and continues.

"During my break, I read an article about a candidate I had not heard of before this election, Westyn Hale. Hale, who is running as an independent, comes across as quite charming. It seems he has combined ideas from both the Republican and Democratic parties to create his platform, incorporating a populist approach. However, trying to please everyone is not an effective strategy in an election. Candidates need to take a clear stance and be principled in their beliefs. Based on his platform, it appears that Mr. Hale lacks those principles."

Paul's voice intensifies as he speaks into the microphone.

"People, please don't be fooled! This Hale guy is trying to deceive the public with an idea that could split the two major parties. If we were on Wall Street, we'd say he's trying to corner the market. If the Republican candidate receives thirty-three percent of the vote, and the Democratic candidate also receives thirty-three percent, the Independent candidate needs to secure only thirty-four percent to win the popular vote. Once that happens, the election will be up for grabs! Hey, if you don't believe me, go back and check out the election of 1984."

Paul takes another sip of his coffee as he continues.

"The Liberal Party is lucky to have a Democrat on the ticket who has endorsed most of our platform. He will be a true people's candidate and will promote policies that support the working class. Let's not get it twisted: We need every vote to win this election. We can't afford to have a Republican in office who favors the business community or a vague Independent who isn't clear on his beliefs. We must be purposeful, focused, and determined to lead this Democratic candidate to victory. That can happen only if you vote for a principled candidate who upholds liberal values. That, my friends, is the Democrat!"

Paul lowers his voice as Rochelle signals for a break.

"WPROG family, I'm sorry. We must take a hard break. We'll be right back!"

Surrounded by the sounds of the city streets, Tony prepares to connect with millions of loyal followers.

"Ladies and gentlemen, my name is Tony Stravell, and I'm the voice of the number one podcast in the nation, *The Gray Forum*. A platform that is unfiltered, unrestricted, and uncompromised. Before we begin, please stay tuned until the end of the program. I want to share an eventful restaurant experience I recently had.

"But first, I have a special guest on the phone. It's Westyn Hale, who is running as an Independent and turning heads with his success in this election.

"Mr. Hale, how are you doing?"

"Tony, I'm doing fine, and I'm glad to be on your show."

"I know your time is limited, so let's get right to it. I saw the interview you gave last night as you left a restaurant. It appears that you were taken aback by the reporter. Do you think he was trying to ambush you politically?"

"Yes, sir. The reporter approached me, assuming I was trying to avoid explaining my political positions. I have been open with the media since the start of my campaign; however, it was only after I made it past the primaries that the media began to take me seriously."

"Did he seem to have other motives, or did he genuinely appear interested in your campaign?"

"There's no doubt he was trying to trap me so he could get a headline or find something sensational to report on social media."

"You named five topics in your platform that you hope will resonate with the voters. Please explain why you think these issues are important."

"Each of the five points focuses on specific areas for which the public expressed their concerns, such as lowering taxes so families can have more money in their pockets, fixing health care so a family does not have to file for bankruptcy to pay medical bills, or making education affordable so a teen in

Alabama can have the same educational opportunities and upward mobility as a teen in New York."

"That sounds good, but I did not hear anything about homeownership."

"I specifically left that out because many factors contribute to the rising cost of homes. No single office can control all the elements related to homeownership. However, we can prioritize this issue in policy discussions to ensure that market stakeholders are monitored and held accountable."

"Sounds like you don't have a specific answer to this issue."

"Come on, Tony. There isn't just one solution to this issue. The housing industry is a complex, multifaceted sector. How can the government intervene in the housing market without causing financial instability across the economy? This is the critical challenge we must address when regulating the housing market."

Tony is dissatisfied with Hale's response and is prepared to ask a follow-up question, but he glances at Rob, who points at his watch, and decides to end the interview there.

"Mr. Hale, I know you're busy, so I appreciate your time. Thank you for calling in."

"No problem, Tony. Your questions were interesting and sparked a light in my thinking. Thank you for having me. Have a great day."

Tony observes Rob as he waits for a sign that Hale is off the air. Seconds later, he gets the nod and continues.

"Ladies and gentlemen, that was candidate Westyn Hale on the phone, and I appreciate the time he took to answer some questions. Listen, we need to take a short break, but stay tuned . . . I've got a restaurant story that will blow your mind!"

5

Time to Shine

I n the months leading up to the election, tensions escalate as all three candidates fiercely compete for public support. Unlike in previous elections, no debates were held because the candidates could not agree on a format. The news media expressed frustration over the situation, as the candidates declined to be interviewed, fearing that any negative coverage could jeopardize their momentum.

One day, as Hale exits his campaign office, he pauses to speak with a group of podcasters waiting outside for an interview. However, before he can address them, his adviser pulls him aside.

"Westyn, these guys look familiar. Aren't these the same podcasters we spent a ton of money on, advertising on their shows?"

Hale smiles and looks at his adviser.

"Yes, we spent thousands flooding their podcasts and other popular social media platforms with ads, persuading their listeners to support my candidacy."

Hale's adviser looks concerned.

"I understand that, but doesn't it look somewhat questionable that the podcasters who are asking you questions are paid by you?"

Unconcerned, Hale shrugs his shoulders.

"Social media is still relatively new to me, and I'm not entirely clear on the ethical rules this country has regarding its use. However, I can tell you this: My understanding is that social media platforms are eager for advertising dollars and attention. They represent an underrepresented and underserved community with which politicians have yet to engage. I may not know what is legal or not; that's your area of expertise. But if our strategy works, we will inform the uninformed, sway the popular vote, influence the Electoral College, and shock the world!"

Hale's adviser smiles, then gazes at him with curiosity.

"By the way, how did these podcasters know we would be leaving the office at this time?"

Hale turns, scans the crowd, then turns back toward his adviser.

"I don't know. It must have been leaked online somehow."

Hale looks at his adviser with a cunning smile as he walks toward the crowd.

"Good afternoon, everyone. I have a few minutes to share my thoughts. Both of my opponents are now focused on the economy, budget deficits, and inflation. However, both establishment parties have had opportunities to address the bloated budget and the national debt, but they have done nothing."

Hale turns to his adviser for confirmation, and his adviser looks back, nodding in agreement.

"What happened to the officials who promised to cut the budget? What happened to the politicians who warned that their children would be burdened with debt for years if nothing was done? Where is the accountability, and where is the outrage?"

As Hale's words become more intense, he pauses before pointing to the growing audience.

"Friends, how much longer will you be deceived? How long will your vote support a candidate who flips their stance once in office? People, when will you wake up and see they don't have your best interests at heart?"

Hale energizes the crowd with his impressive off-the-cuff speech skills.

"When you vote for me, you support a five-point plan to strengthen our nation and improve your quality of life. You endorse a tax policy that puts more money in your hands now, not a tax credit that will leave your family struggling until you file taxes.

"You support a policy that will dismantle the current educational caste system, emphasizing that when you uplift and educate the underprivileged, you strengthen the nation.

"You vote for a basic government-sponsored health care plan that will ensure that our people are healthy enough to pursue their dreams. I said it before, and I'll repeat it. A healthy nation is a strong nation!"

Something resonates with the crowd as they begin responding to Hale's proposals, much like congregants listening to a sermon in a Baptist church.

"When we strengthen our military, it's like putting up a fence around our property. Some neighbors, like countries, have no boundaries, and showing strength keeps them away. Why is this necessary? Because the most valuable thing in your home and nation is your family, and they must be protected."

The crowd hangs on every word as Hale shows his genius in connecting national issues to personal concerns.

"You vote for me because family values are vital to the social fabric of this great country. Who said that the established political parties have a stronghold on family values? Although we're a nation enriched with diverse cultures and traditions, we remain one nation, indivisible, with liberty and justice for all."

A potential interview has evolved into a rally. Hale smiles and looks out over the crowd.

"Listen, I'm not pretending I can do everything for everyone; however, I know I can do these five things, and that, my friends, is more than any established politician has accomplished in the last fifty years! Thank you and have a great day!"

The crowd cheers as Hale waves, gets into his car, and smiles at his adviser.

"See? They love me! It's only a matter of time before we achieve our purpose here."

It's Election Day, and the excitement in the air is intense. The campaigning, interviews, and fundraising have wrapped up, and the polls are full of eager voters ready to cast their ballots.

Sitting at his desk in the booth, Mitch is ready to do his part to encourage his audience to vote.

"This is the moment we've been waiting for. Of the three candidates running for office, the Republican is the best choice to tackle all our problems. He is a man who believes in Christian values. He supports the business community and capitalism as the economic engine that will lead this nation to greatness. He upholds moral standards and rejects the idea that everyone's truth is the truth. He believes this is the greatest nation in the world, one that guarantees freedom of speech, assembly, and religion. Oh, and let's not forget the right to keep and bear arms. He may not be a conservative, but he's a better option than the Democrat or Independent on the ticket."

Mitch glances at Jake, who flashes the break sign.

"Listen, family, just vote Republican! It's the godly thing to do."

Jake stares at him, surprised.

"Godly?" he mouths.

Mitch smiles.

"Yes, I said it! We'll be back after this short break."

While Mitch strongly supports the Republican candidate, Paul remains just as dedicated to the Democratic candidate.

"Folks, this is it! I'm tired and drained from this entire election process. I'm exhausted from trying to convince you that the Democrat in this race is much better than the Conservative and the Independent. I'm tired of telling you that an all-inclusive nation is a great nation. I'm tired of saying that the strength of this nation depends on the health of its people. I'm tired of old men in Congress telling women what they can or cannot do. This nation's potential is limitless; however, the opportunity to realize that potential must be available to everyone. The race for happiness isn't just for those who can afford running shoes; it's for all who strive to do more and be more in the greatest nation in the world!

"Friends, as we go out to vote, I'm not concerned about the Republican candidate; my main worry is Candidate Hale." By now, most of us have likely figured out his strategy. He plans to split the popular vote among three candidates and use that victory to influence the Electoral College. Remember, the winner of the election is not necessarily the candidate who receives the most popular votes; it's the candidate who garners the most votes from the Electoral College. Who is the Electoral College? That, my friends, is a topic for another discussion."

Paul looks up and sees Rochelle signal for a hard break.

"The key point to remember is that Mr. Hale needs two hundred seventy electoral votes to win the presidency. Folks, we'll be right back after this commercial break. In the meantime, get out and vote!"

The afternoon gradually transitions into evening as traffic on Eleventh Avenue in New York City begins to pick up. Meanwhile, Tony is in his studio, discussing the national election with his audience.

"Ladies and gentlemen, we're in the final stretch of a national election that started more than a year ago. Recently, I interviewed Westyn Hale, who has made an impressive run for office with his five-point plan for the nation. Honestly, I didn't think he went far enough in explaining his platform; however, he has somehow managed to win the hearts of the working class with his clear proposals. His connection with the public is evident in the millions of dollars he received, which allowed him to reject corporate funding."

Tony looks across the room at Rob as he continues.

"Do you understand what that means? It means he can create policies based on what is right, rather than what corporations expect. Ladies and gentlemen, that's justice, that's liberty, and that, my friends, is freedom from corporate oppression!"

Tony realizes that he is getting fired up and lowers his tone.

"Somehow, Hale has adjusted his platform so that major national issues, which usually bore the average person, are now connected to their personal lives. My friends, this approach has been tested before, but never on this scale or with such success."

Tony looks at Rob.

With this in mind, I encourage you to vote for the non-establishment candidate, Westyn Hale."

Rob holds up the sign for a break.

"Family, thank you for listening to the number one podcast in the nation, *The Gray Forum*. Please support my podcast, and remember what you see on the surface is meant for you to see. We'll be right back after a word from our sponsors."

6
The Jitters

The evening remains young, and anticipation lingers in the air as the nation eagerly awaits the election results. Mitch is home, lounging on the couch with Jean, captivated by the local news. Suddenly, the national news cuts in, heightening the tension.

"Good evening, this is a special report from the National News Center in New York. This is election night! The polls are closed, and our reporters are verifying sources and gathering real-time election updates. We'll keep you informed of the results as the night goes on. Now, we'll return you to your regularly scheduled programming."

Mitch looks at his wife and smiles.

"Jean, this election should be an easy win for the Republican candidate. Our values, our commitment, and our traditions represent what this nation stands for. It would take a miracle for our candidate to lose, and as you know, that's not possible because we have God on our side."

Jean nods in agreement but adds, "I agree; however, Westyn Hale presented a strong anti-establishment platform that was impressive and resonated with voters."

Aggravated, Mitch stares at his wife. "So, you're telling me you voted for Hale?"

Jean glares at Mitch incredulously.

"Are you kidding? His platform is attractive, yet his values are not my values."

Mitch turns to his wife.

"Wow, you scared me for a moment. You know what the Bible says: 'As for me and my house, we will vote Republican.'"

Jean looks at Mitch with curiosity as he grins mischievously.

"What did you just say? The Bible does not say that."

Mitch sneers as he watches the election results on television.

"Mine does! It's called the CIV: the Conservative International Version."

Astonished, Jean looks at Mitch and shakes her head.

"Really, Mitch . . . you've got issues!"

Back at his Upper East Side apartment, an uneasy Paul sits at the dining room table, preparing to eat dinner while anxiously watching the election results. Looking around and somewhat on edge, Paul looks at Kelly.

"Hey, Kelly, where are the boys?"

Kelly glances at Paul, wondering why he's asking her.

"I don't know. They should be in their rooms."

Paul is surprised by her laid-back attitude.

"Did you check on them to see what they're doing?"

Kelly walks by Paul as she sets the table. "No. Why don't you go in there and check? Can't you see that I'm preparing dinner?"

Annoyed, Paul turns to Kelly.

"You know, when I was growing up, I wasn't allowed to stay in my room all day. In fact, I was made to go outside and play. So, let me ask you a question."

Kelly hears his tone and is not happy with the direction the conversation is taking as Paul continues.

"Why do we let the boys stay in their rooms all day? I wasn't allowed to keep my door closed until I turned eighteen. Before that, there was no privacy in my house except for the door to my parents' room."

Kelly rolls her eyes as she listens patiently to Paul's rant.

"Right now, we're watching election results that could change their lives, and they're completely oblivious to what's happening!"

Kelly grimaces at Paul as she serves dinner and sits at the dining room table.

"Paul, we've raised these kids all these years, giving them the freedom to make good choices, and now you're worried? Come on, we taught our kids well."

Paul looks at Kelly as he bites into his dinner.

"Really? Then why did I catch them smoking marijuana on the balcony? They know my rules, yet they still took the risk of getting caught. I'm just worried about their ability to make the right choices for the future."

Kelly stares at Paul, wondering where all this energy is coming from.

"Young people today are trying to find their own paths in life. If we pressure them too much about the path we think they should take, we risk stifling their creativity and growth."

Paul glares at Kelly skeptically.

"Kelly, is that what you learned about young people after twenty years of being an educator? Are they genuinely seeking their own path, or are they just smoking pot and looking for the easy way out? I consider myself a liberal, but being liberal doesn't mean we aren't responsible. When did we reach a point where young people no longer need guidance and discipline? I recognize the value of creativity, but shouldn't we make sure they channel that energy into something productive?"

Frustrated, Paul jumps up from the table and walks down the hall toward his sons' rooms.

Kelly sees him and shouts, "Paul, where are you going? Your food is going to get cold!"

"I'm going to check on my sons and remind them that when dinner is served, I expect them to be at the table, even if they're not hungry. This way, we can stay connected to what's happening in their lives."

Kelly shakes her head and continues eating her dinner while the TV plays in the background.

"Good evening, this is a special report from the National News Center in New York. Our reporters are actively gathering real-time information on the election results. As of the hour, the latest polling indicates that this race is too close to call. Stay tuned for updates throughout the night. Now, back to your regularly scheduled programming."

Although most traditional radio hosts have left the airwaves, a nationally recognized podcaster is just now wrapping up his broadcast.

"Ladies and gentlemen, this concludes my podcast on election night. My name is Tony Stravell, and remember: What you see on the surface is only what you are meant to see. Have a good night."

Tony packs up his bags, speaks to Rob for a few minutes, and goes to his car. While on the road, he calls his girlfriend, Nicole.

"Hey, Nicole, what's going on?"

Nicole turns around in her bed as her voice cracks. "Everything is good, sweetheart. How are you?"

Tony has a big smile on his face as he looks forward to the evening.

"I'm doing well, and it's election night. Listen, I'm on my way to pick you up so we can grab something to eat and watch the election results."

Nicole sits up in bed.

"Sorry, Tony, but that's not going to happen tonight. I don't feel like hanging out."

Tony is caught off guard and wonders what's going on.

"We get together every election night. A major part of my podcast's success is reporting on current events, and you have been a key contributor to that success ever since you called in to my show seven years ago. I don't understand."

Nicole turns on the light in her room. "Listen, Jason confided in me about a personal issue concerning his girlfriend, and he's feeling depressed. It seems he's going through a tough time, and I want to be here for him in case he needs some encouragement."

Tony gets confused and almost has an accident as he pulls his vehicle over to the side of the road.

"Are you serious? What about me? I'm upset because I won't be able to see you tonight. You're about to break a seven-year election tradition for a twenty-eight-year-old man who's heartbroken, unemployed, doesn't pay any bills, and lives with his mom? Honestly, I don't even get how he has a girlfriend, considering he has no money!"

Nicole is upset at Tony's response. "Hey, Tony! Can you show some empathy and compassion? Not everyone suppresses their emotions and knows how to man up as you do!"

Tony is still parked on the side of the road.

"Nicole, there are times when a man needs some empathy, and times when a man must hold on to his emotions. A man who has not learned how to conquer his feelings will act impulsively, and that, my love, is a dangerous man!"

Tony hears nothing on the other end of the phone and should have stopped while he was ahead, but he is in talk-show mode and keeps ranting.

"Your son is a respectful young man. However, when will he be able to make decisions about his personal life without his mother stepping in?"

Nicole gets out of bed to make sure Tony clearly understands what she is about to say. "Jason is my only son, and if he needs my input, I'll give it to him—whether you like it or not!"

This isn't the first time Nicole and Tony have discussed this. They've argued about Jason's lack of ambition for years.

"Nicole, Jason spends all his time in the basement playing video games and posting on social media, with his main goal in life being to become an influencer. I've sent him plenty of job opportunities over the years, and he hasn't acted on any of them. It almost seems like he thinks that working a nine-to-five job is beneath him. Listen, sweetheart, I'm just trying to do my part in helping him become a responsible man."

Nicole closes the door to her room.

"Tony, with all due respect, that's not your job! It's my responsibility to guide my son into adulthood. I am a single mother, not by choice, doing the best I can with what I have."

Tony sits back in his seat, realizes the conversation is getting heated, and lowers his tone.

"Yes, I know you're strong and doing your best, and I applaud that, but when will you accept that even you have limits, and that it takes a village?"

The silence on the line is nerve-racking. Tony realizes that he may have won the argument, but he has lost the evening. He puts his phone on speaker, pulls away from the curb, makes a U-turn, and heads home.

Frustrated, Nicole stays silent as she turns off the lights in her room and lies back down on her bed. Knowing that Tony will not hang up his phone until she does, she picks up the phone from her bed.

"Tony, I've had enough. I didn't ask for criticism of my parenting skills; I just wanted to let you know I was unavailable tonight."

Tony now regrets the entire conversation.

"Come on, Nicole, that wasn't a rebuke; it was simply a comment made with love."

Tony is doing his best to salvage what remains of the night.

"So, is that it for the night?"

Nicole says, "Yes, that's it. Have a good night, Tony."

And without giving Tony a chance to say good night, Nicole hangs up and tosses around to try to go to sleep.

Just a few minutes from home, Tony turns on the radio while searching for parking.

"Good evening. This is a special report from the National News Center in New York. In an unexpected development that is shaking up the political establishment, we're declaring Westyn Hale the winner of the election, with ninety-five percent of the polls reporting. For only the second time in this nation's history, an Independent candidate has secured victory, capturing thirty-five percent of the popular vote and a majority of the electoral votes."

Tony can't believe what he is hearing as the announcer repeats the astonishing news.

"Once again, for those just tuning in, Westyn Hale is on track for a major upset and a surprising victory in this nation's election. There has been no comment from either the Democratic or Republican parties. Stay tuned for the latest updates on this unprecedented win."

Still searching for a parking spot, Tony is stunned and whispers to himself.

"This is the beginning of something big!"

7

Speechless

It is the day after the election, and the atmosphere crackles with tension as Mitch's voice booms through the studio, setting the stage for what promises to be an intense show.

"Ladies and gentlemen, what the hell happened last night?"

Mitch directs his attention to Jake as he speaks over the air.

"Just to let you know, I'm not taking any calls until I feel like taking calls!"

Jake nods in agreement.

"Folks, am I dreaming or having a nightmare? We're a nation built on a two-party system that has lasted for over two hundred years. Yet through some out-of-this-world miracle, Westyn Hale has been elected the most powerful leader in the world?"

Mitch scratches his head as his frustration grows.

"No Independent candidate has ever received more than nineteen percent in a national election, and now we have an unknown entity in charge." I want to know who vetted him and how he managed to win the primaries. The word is that this Hale guy has no skeletons in his closet. Someone isn't doing their job! There are always skeletons! Wake me up and tell me this is a nightmare!"

Mitch, visibly aggravated. Looks at Jake.

"Hey, why are you on the phone? I told you, I'm not taking any calls today. The people don't deserve to talk to me. I told my audience that if they don't vote Republican, they shouldn't vote at all. Why would you vote for an Independent candidate who has no core values, no principles, and no spiritual convictions? I don't understand it!"

Jake jumps in with his opinion.

"Hey, Mitch, maybe it was Hale's five-point platform that resonated with the people? It seemed to be simple and easy to understand."

An irritated Mitch looks at Jake and shouts, "Hold on! Hold on! . . . Whose name is headlined in this show?"

Jake hesitates after realizing he should have stayed silent.

"Mitch Corvane."

Mitch locks his eyes on Jake while walking toward the glass partition.

"And who is the number one syndicated talk show host in the nation?"

Jake hesitantly replies, "Mitch Corvane."

Mitch points at Jake and screams, "So, when I want your opinion, I'll ask for it. Otherwise, I suggest you shut the hell up and keep your unwelcome thoughts to yourself!"

There's a moment of silence as both men glare at each other angrily through the glass partition. To make matters worse, Jake looks at his monitor and realizes they are still live and on the air. Humiliated, he signals for the break, starts packing his bag, and heads for the exit.

Mitch notices the break sign and grabs the mic from his desk, regretfully watching Jake leave.

"Ladies and gentlemen, I apologize for what you just heard. The frustration of this election got the best of me. Stay where you are, and don't go anywhere; we'll be right back."

Mitch turns off his mike, takes off his headphones, and mumbles out loud.

"Lord, I messed up!"

He then bolts out of the studio, runs down the hall, and goes after his producer.

Across town, in a dimly lit studio, Paul is also stunned, grappling with the shock of the unexpected election results. The atmosphere is heavy with tension, and the weight of the moment lingers in the air like a thick fog. He stares at the microphone before him, still struggling to process the harsh reality that his candidate lost.

"Ladies and gentlemen, in my twenty years on broadcast radio, I have never seen election results like this. Who the heck is Westyn Hale? Oh, I'm sorry, President-elect Hale. Where did he come from, and how did he slip under our radar?"

Paul adjusts the microphone closer to his face as he continues speaking:

"Hale's trying to be everything to everyone. He has a little bit of conservatism, some liberalism, and a tad bit of Independent policies packaged neatly so that the public believes he is the people's politician."

Paul stares at Rochelle through the booth.

"Is this what the people want?"

Rochelle picks up her microphone and shrugs her shoulders. "I guess so, Paul. It was only five political points, but somehow, it resonated with the people."

Paul slams his hand on his desk.

"You know, when an unknown candidate can toss out some obtuse policies and they stick, I think it might be time for me to hang it up!"

Paul's words surprise Rochelle.

"What do you mean?"

Paul paces the studio floor as he continues.

"I'm telling you that times are changing. Traditional radio has fallen behind podcasts, and social media platforms are quickly becoming the voice of the people."

Feeling despondent, Paul picks up the water bottle from his desk and takes a sip.

"The number of people following social media influencers is staggering. One superstar can garner as many as one hundred twenty-eight million followers on social media. It's only a matter of time before a political issue arises, and these influencers realize their true power, using it to gain political influence. Currently, they seem complacent and comfortable operating in their own worlds. However, if they ever recognize their potential, the established powers in this nation will be in serious trouble!"

Rochelle reflects on his statements and is concerned.

"Hey, Paul, I just want to say I think you're being too hard on yourself. While you do have influence, you don't have control over the Democratic Party or its agenda. Still, voices like yours are important in a society that needs reminders of its identity."

Paul smiles at Rochelle and holds in a chuckle.

"Maybe it's just my perception, but sometimes, it feels like everything I've worked for over the past twenty years doesn't matter to this new generation. To make matters worse, even my kids, who used to respect everything I said, recently sneaked and smoked weed in my home."

Paul sits down at his desk and stares at his monitor. An uneasy, unusual silence fills the booth and the airwaves as he remains quiet. Rochelle, realizing that Paul is having a moment, waits patiently. Then, suddenly, Paul breaks his silence and speaks to Rochelle.

"All right, that's enough of us sharing our personal insights and boring our audience. Let's open the phone lines and hear from our listeners. I want to know their thoughts as we navigate through this unbelievable election."

"Good afternoon, everyone. This is Tony Stravell in New York City, and you're listening to *The Gray Forum*. I'm looking forward to a lively discussion about the interesting results of last night's national election. Let me be up-front: When I interviewed Westyn Hale, I wasn't fully impressed with his agenda. He presented five political points, but didn't explain how he plans to implement them. Even when I asked him a simple question about housing, he hesitated and said he had limited control over the market. So, for now, all we have is a five-point plan that supposedly will fix the country's problems."

Tony leans back in his chair and takes a sip of water while watching Rob, who is on the other side of the living room–style studio. With a look of concern on his face, Tony gazes at the microphone.

"Family, I'm not going to lie to you. Although the five points President-elect Hale proposed sound impressive, something about their simplicity and his background doesn't sit right with me. So, even though I'm an independent at heart, I'm holding back judgment and waiting to see how he plans to enforce his policies."

Tony looks at Rob and shakes his head.

"The results of this election have been a welcome surprise to me. However, a bigger question arises: Are we prepared for an Independent candidate who will make decisions based on a five-point policy that has not been tested over time?"

Tony winces as he recalls his question.

"Keep in mind that this candidate is independent and not beholden to any established constituency. This independence can be a strength, enabling him to challenge the current political structure. However, it also comes with the risk of unpredictability, which may result in a lack of accountability to the people."

Rob puts up a sign indicating the need for a break.

"Remember, when it comes to politics, nothing is what it seems on the surface. It's the details beneath that shape our destinies. This is what we await from President-elect Hale: not just smooth rhetoric, but actions that show he's serious about keeping his promises."

Tony pushes his chair back as he goes on a break.

"Ladies and gentlemen, this is Tony Stravell from *The Gray Forum*, and you're listening to our live election podcast from New York City. Don't go anywhere; we'll be right back."

8

One Hundred Days

It's a beautiful day in the nation's capital, and at the base of its steps, a podium has been set up for President-elect Hale to hold his first news conference. He arrives confidently, walking toward the platform, one week after his election victory. Surrounded by his campaign workers and advisers, he stands at the podium, adjusts his microphone, and addresses the media.

"Good afternoon, everyone. Can everyone hear me?"

The crowd shouts, "Yes!"

President-elect Hale continues.

"This is a historic day for the working-class people of our nation. Our campaign has made the impossible possible. Unfortunately, many in the media failed to recognize the brilliance of our agenda and did not give us a chance."

Hale scans the crowd, glances at the media, and shouts, "I just have one question . . . How do you like me now?"

A roar erupts from Hale's supporters as he continues.

"We made a promise to deliver on specific policies during the campaign, and I intend to fulfill those promises with or without Congress's help. The people voted for change, and I promise you, change is coming. Some believed that my platform, which outlined five major policies, was just a gimmick. However, I want to clarify that it's anything but that."

President-elect Hale adjusts his tie and straightens his jacket as he reminds the media why he won the election.

"First, my proposal to lower taxes for the middle class and corporations remains in effect to promote a respectful fiscal relationship between the two. A negative relationship between the public and the business community can lead only to economic chaos, benefiting no one. An understanding must be reached so that the working class can appreciate the efforts of the business class, and the business class can respect the working class."

Hale's supporters and advisers stand behind him, clapping enthusiastically.

"Second, education should be accessible to everyone, not just the wealthy. I am committed to ensuring that anyone pursuing higher education to lift their family out of generational poverty can do so. Whether through student loans, grants, or college subsidies, the government must take the lead in promoting education now and in the future."

Again, Hale's supporters and advisers clap energetically, delaying President-elect Hale from continuing.

"Third, how can anyone pursue their dreams if they're not in good health? We live in the world's strongest economy, so why can't we establish a basic government health care plan for everyone? Such a plan would protect our people from sickness and disease, as well as heartache, pain, and the financial burden of medical bills and debt. No family in our great nation should have to choose between putting food on the table and going to the doctor! Now, I'm not sure what a basic health care plan would entail; yet I'm confident that a government plan will not infringe on those seeking a more comprehensive plan from the private sector."

President-elect Hale pauses and looks over the crowd.

"Look, we need to take action. I mentioned this during my campaign, and I'll repeat it: We can't be a strong nation unless we're a healthy nation!"

Once again, a roar of exuberance and excitement fills the air as President-elect Hale raises his hand for calm.

"Fourth, ladies and gentlemen, how can we have a strong economy and a strong nation without a robust military? Funding is crucial for maintaining the strength of our armed forces. During the campaign, I emphasized that the stronger we are, the weaker our enemies become, and I stand by that statement. We do not live in a vacuum. If this nation is attacked, we all face the threat, and the most vulnerable among us—the poor, the underprivileged, and the disenfranchised— will suffer the most. I assure you that this will not happen under my watch!"

An elated shout of approval comes from the crowd as he winds down his speech.

"Finally, I believe in traditional family values; however, I understand that we have the freedom to make choices, and I respect that. Therefore, I will not judge others or force my personal beliefs through my policies. Still, as the young people say, we must keep it real. Whether we like it or not, we're all judged in some way or another. However, our objective should always be to judge others by the content of their character."

Hale glanced back at his adviser, and a confident smile spread across his face as he concluded his speech.

"For those who feel overlooked, marginalized, or rejected, I offer you hope. A hope that does not come from humanity but from a higher source. A source that sees past your human flaws and understands what your critics often overlook—your heart!"

Hale's supporters erupt in cheers and applause as he finishes his speech. As the clapping continues, Hale turns and whispers to his adviser, "Do I have to take questions?"

"You should because it's the way it is done here, but the straight answer to your question is no."

Hale whispers back. "Then forget them!"

Hale then turns back to the podium as the media raises their hands for questions.

"I want to thank the media for attending my first news conference. You have been patient, tolerant, and a wonderful audience. Have a great day!"

The media is stunned, and their faces show a blend of surprise and frustration as President-elect Hale walks away. As he heads to his vehicle, Hale glances at his adviser.

"They didn't believe in me before, but by the end, they'll see the light."

Hale's adviser chimes in, "I agree."

Two months later, the swearing-in ceremony is over, and President Hale, along with his adviser, Mr. Bishop, steps through the grand entrance of the Presidential Office. President Hale takes a moment to appreciate the scene as sunlight streams through the windows. His adviser shares in the wonder, admiring the decor and the historic paintings that adorn the room.

"Mr. President, while the decor in this room is attractive, it reflects the previous administration. You already have the funding allocated and the opportunity to renovate it during your time in office."

President Hale observes the room's ambience in silence.

"Sir, past presidents have ordered renovations for the Presidential Office. It's expected that you'll continue this trend."

Annoyed, the president turns to his adviser.

"You see, Mr. Bishop, that's your problem. We just got here, and you're already eager to follow trends. We're not here to follow trends; we're here on a mission, one that will ensure the continuation of this construct."

President Hale walks away, continuing to marvel at the history portrayed in his new office.

"Leave the decor as it is, and while you're at it, provide me with all previous executive orders issued by my predecessors that can effectively support my five-point policy. Since these orders have already been tested, we won't need to worry about potential court challenges."

Mr. Bishop looks at the president, who continues to survey the room.

"Mr. President, that is a monumental task that will take some time. How long do I have to get you this information?"

The president turns around.

"I want to demonstrate to the public what good leadership can accomplish in its first hundred days in office."

Mr. Bishop looks at the president with concern.

"One hundred days, sir?"

The president gazes at his adviser with eyes full of expectation.

"Yes, one hundred days. Is that a problem?"

Mr. Bishop looks at the president.

"No, sir. I'll have the staff address this immediately. Anything else, sir?"

The president turns and runs his hand along the wood of his desk before taking a seat.

"Mr. Bishop, every president before me has made campaign promises that they did not fulfill. We'll do everything in our power to implement our agenda. If we're unable to achieve this, it will hinder our efforts to fulfill our purpose."

Mr. Bishop listens attentively and nods in agreement.

"Mr. President, so, how do we begin to accomplish our goals within a political structure that resists change?"

The president rises from his desk and paces the floor, burdened by the weight of his campaign promises as he considers his next move.

"Mr. Bishop, this week I want you to contact the leaders of the House and Senate and provide them with an outline of my plans. I need to find out how many support my plan and how many oppose it."

Mr. Bishop curiously looks at the president.

"Sir, the issue isn't the policies, but rather how they will be implemented and funded. Given our current budget deficit, you will likely face challenges."

Aggravated, the president looks at his adviser.

"Mr. Bishop, didn't I tell you that we don't follow trends? We make them!"

His adviser responds, "Yes, sir."

President Hale raises his voice in frustration.

"Therefore, I suggest you not worry about how things will be done. We came here for a purpose. Just start the process. Do you understand me?"

The president's adviser is taken aback by his tone.

"Yes, sir."

Mr. Bishop proceeds to walk out of the office.

"Have a good day, Mr. President."

Silence fills the room as Mr. Bishop leaves the office. Frustrated by his adviser's concerns, President Hale grabs a pen and paper to outline his plan. Lost in thought, he is determined to turn his ambitious promises into concrete proposals that will lead the nation toward its destiny.

Two weeks later, the president is in his office, working on his policies, when Mr. Bishop enters.

"Mr. President, how are you doing today?"

President Hale makes eye contact with his adviser. "I'm doing well. What's on your mind?"

Mr. Bishop paces.

"I'm working on a strategy to submit our policies to Congress. One idea is to introduce our five-point plan in stages, presenting each point individually. This method can be effective because it allows us to track responses at each stage and make adjustments before proceeding to the next. Every time we get feedback on a policy we present, we can adjust the next phase to improve its chances of acceptance."

The president nods, impressed. "Not bad, Mr. Bishop, for someone new to this process. However, shouldn't we focus on the overall package rather than breaking it into individual phases? The system here is quite complex. With five separate petitions, Congress has five chances to undermine our plan. If we combine everything into one comprehensive bill, then if one part of the policy is approved, all of our policies will pass together."

The president stands and joins Mr. Bishop on the blue wool carpet, which features the Presidential Seal, as he continues.

"Mr. Bishop, I appreciate your perspective, but I prefer my approach because it lets me leverage my influence with Congress more effectively. By addressing all my policies at once, I can present a bold package rather than petitioning Congress multiple times to pass individual bills. Following your approach could make my presidency appear weak, and that is unacceptable."

Mr. Bishop, frustrated that his plan has been dismissed, appears bothered and irritated.

"Whatever you say, Mr. President."

The president looks at Mr. Bishop and reluctantly smiles.

"All right, let's get busy developing my plan to submit to Congress."

9

Backlash

The bumper music fades into the background as Mitch's voice echoes with anticipation, signaling the start of his show.

"Ladies and gentlemen, my name is Mitch Corvane, and I'm the number one conservative talk show host in the nation. Now, let's skip all the formalities and get right to the point. You wouldn't believe what this newly elected, inexperienced president has done! Instead of going through the legislative process to achieve his goals, he sent a list of demands to the Senate and House, attempting to force elected leaders to accept his policies without congressional deliberation. This guy doesn't understand how the process works, and he is making enemies with the people he needs to pass his agenda!"

Mitch glances at Jake.

"Who is President Hale, and what made him think he could present a list of demands to Congress? He's a simple man with a simple mind, promoting simple policies. It's just as simple as that!"

Jake can't help but smile as Mitch continues.

"The president discussed the need to lower taxes, which I agree with; however, he fails to specify the fiscal details required to prevent inflation. He aims to improve educational opportunities for everyone, but two weeks after his plan for funding education was posted, colleges increased their tuition in anticipation of a financial gain."

Mitch looks at his notes.

"He also wants to increase military spending, which I have no objection to; however, where will the funding come from if he significantly cuts taxes? His plan to implement government-funded health care poses a threat to our economic structure, as this could undermine our current medical system."

Mitch sips on a glass of water as he continues.

"While he claims to be a man who believes in a higher power, I find it hard to believe that he truly believes in the teachings of the Scriptures. He presents himself as a politician for the people, claiming to have all the answers, rather than acknowledging that his power and strength come from above. I recall a Scripture that says, 'It's not by power or might, but by my Spirit.' Thus says the Lord."

Mitch bangs on his desk as Jake calls for a break.

"If President Hale continues to implement his simplistic policies without understanding their significant impact on the nation, I fear we may reach a point of no return. As many of you know, I'm unapologetically a Christian and hold my beliefs with conviction and honor. Despite differing opinions,

I'm strongly convinced that, given everything happening, we're living in the last days."

Mitch picks up the microphone from his desk and leans back in his chair.

"Hearing that, some of you might think I'm an alarmist, but let me ask you this: How long can a society survive when its foundational and spiritual order is twisted by a culture determined to do things its own way? I know that many of my listeners are fiscal and social conservatives who may not share my beliefs. Still, I encourage you to consider this: Science and the laws of nature teach us that every beginning has an end. If their theory is true, a day of reckoning is coming, and I believe that artificial intelligence will play a key role in it."

Mitch smiles as he drinks his water.

"Let's hope that when that time comes, we find ourselves on the right side of that transition. So, fasten your seat belts, ladies and gentlemen! With this president at the helm and his policies shrouded in uncertainty, we're in for an interesting ride to the finish. We'll be right back after a word from our sponsors."

"Ladies and gentlemen, we're back from a commercial break, and you're listening to the number one nationally syndicated liberal talk show host in the nation, Paul Vorbont. President Hale has presented a list of policy objectives for Congress to consider, and after reviewing them, I feel both encouraged and conflicted."

Paul drinks some coffee as he continues.

"The president wants to lower taxes on the working class and the business community. That sounds good; however, why reduce taxes on a business class that doesn't pay taxes, anyway? After deductions and all sorts of write-offs they're entitled to, they end up paying less in taxes than the average working-class individual."

Paul looks at Rochelle.

"What is even more troubling is the impact of insufficient tax revenue on social services. Social Security, Medicare, and Medicaid are already nearing bankruptcy, and now President Hale might unintentionally be pushing these programs toward financial collapse."

Paul's face reveals his passion as he continues speaking.

"On a brighter note, I agree with the president's proposed health care plan. I believe a basic government plan would be an effective way to provide health care for those most in need. However, I think the president's proposal doesn't go far enough in outlining the services a government health care plan should include. He states that the government will provide basic services, and if you want additional services, you can get them through private insurance."

Paul suspiciously turns and speaks to Rochelle.

"As a result, those with money can access vision and dental care, while the working class is left to bump into people because of poor sight and walk around with bad breath!"

Rochelle chuckles behind the glass as Paul continues.

"It would be amusing if it weren't so serious. Of all the proposals the president made, I noticed no mention of global warming. I wonder why that is. Maybe the issue isn't popular among his constituents. Perhaps he isn't as independent as we thought and is receiving funds from the energy industry, or maybe he doesn't care."

Paul shrugs his shoulders as he stares at Rochelle.

"Maybe it's just me. Am I crazy to say that all inhabitants of this beautiful planet should recognize their role in its health and well-being? Look, even if you don't believe in its science, what's wrong with promoting clean air to breathe, clean water to drink, and maintaining a healthy environment to live in? Friends, I do not consider myself an environmental extremist; however, as far as we know, there are no other planets available for us to live on."

Paul speaks passionately into the microphone as he finishes the last of his coffee.

"I believe global warming is a threat to humanity, and we're witnessing this danger right in front of us. So, please, let's make the most of our time on the planet we call Earth, and take care of it so it will take care of us."

Captivated by Paul's passion, Rochelle applauds from the other side of the glass before signaling him to take a break.

"Ladies and gentlemen, stay right there! We'll be right back after these words from our sponsors."

Paul smiles at Rochelle and gives her a thumbs-up as he makes another cup of coffee and gets ready for his next segment.

The sun slowly sets behind the city skyline while Tony eagerly waits to begin his broadcast. He gets comfortable as the calming sound of jazz fills the air, and he leans into the microphone.

"It's been a beautiful day in New York City, and I was excited and perplexed at the same time as our new president presented his political agenda to Congress."

Tony settles into his seat and continues.

"I support President Hale because he claims to operate independently from the establishment. He owes nothing to outside interests and can craft policies without being influenced by lobbyists or special interest groups. By now, you've likely heard most of his proposals and listened to other talk show hosts discuss his policies. Nonetheless, bear with me as I take a different approach to evaluate his policies, one that goes beyond the surface."

Tony sips some water as he continues.

"Honestly, I'm skeptical about whether the president can keep creating policy without giving in to the pressure of corporate interests. He launched a powerful people's campaign, effectively using social media and other online platforms to engage marginalized and disenfranchised communities. He focused on those who have a voice but are unheard. However, my experience in politics has made me cynical about politicians and the media. I have concluded that what appears on the surface often does not truly reflect reality."

Tony glances at Rob.

"I want to clarify that while I support many of the president's actions, my primary loyalty lies with my listeners.

He has expressed a desire to significantly lower taxes, which may sound appealing; however, we also need to consider the larger issue of spending. I share the same concerns about health care and education. Still, how will he secure the necessary funding for his platform if he does not reduce spending? These questions are ones you will only hear on my show, as we look beneath the surface to uncover the truth."

Tony sips some water as Rob signals for a break.

"Before we go to break, I want to briefly share my views on family values, which President Hale mentioned. I strongly support family values, as long as the family defines them for themselves. I don't believe the government has the right to decide what makes a family or how it should function. After all, their record of handling their own family issues is far from perfect, yet they want to tell me how to run mine?"

Tony grimaces as he thinks about the hypocrisy.

"The president also mentioned a higher source in his address to the media. As you know, I identify as agnostic, which means I don't know whether there's enough evidence to determine if God exists. Now, please don't call my show asking how I formed my beliefs, considering I was raised in the church. I do have faith, but it's in science and the methods created to verify the evidence of truth."

Excited about the topic, Tony continues speaking past the break.

"Based on what we currently know, Earth seems to be a unique planet, but our understanding of space remains limited. With trillions of galaxies, each containing an unknown number of stars, it makes sense that other life-forms exist. I strongly believe that through the monitoring of the universe, we'll ultimately find that we're not alone."

Rob signals for a break as Tony deliberately ignores him again.

"However, I recently learned that the government is working on installing an advanced version of artificial intelligence into our space transmission systems. Once this is complete, it will be impossible to predict what we might discover as we begin transmitting radar signals at unimaginable speeds. The possibilities of contacting other life-forms are truly limitless!"

Tony pauses, glances at Rob, and offers his apologies as he goes to a break.

"Sorry! You're listening to *The Gray Forum* with Tony Stravell, and remember: What you see on the surface is meant for you to see. We'll be right back after a word from our sponsors."

Tony gazes at Rob with regret for not taking the break.

"Sorry, I got a little carried away."

Rob shakes his head in frustration. "No kidding . . ."

10

The Fallout

One year into his term, President Hale is making headway on delivering on his campaign promises. After a lengthy meeting with Congress, where he emphasizes the advantages of his five-point plan, he holds targeted discussions with key power players. During these talks, he emphasizes the importance of federal funding, subtly warning them that losing it could significantly affect their states and their chances for reelection.

Six months later, an unprecedented weekend congressional session approves the president's five-point policy agenda. Unfortunately, despite Hale's promise of transparency, the details of the vote were not made public. Notwithstanding some criticisms, the president's policies have received a notably positive response, with Wall Street reporting increased profits driven by lower taxes and higher consumer spending.

As economic excitement spreads across the country, Mitch enters his home, and Jean greets him with the same optimism.

"Mitch, it's good to see you. How was your day?"

Mitch takes off his jacket and kisses Jean.

"It was one of those days when I had to warn my conservative listeners and colleagues not to get too excited over the boost in the economy."

Mitch takes off his shoes.

"They're going crazy over the stock market, the real estate boom, and corporate profits. I had to remind them that President Hale is an Independent, not a Conservative."

Jean, confused, looks at Mitch as he sits on the couch.

"But isn't it a good thing that the economy is thriving under these new tax cuts? Isn't the tax cut part of the conservative platform?"

Mitch looks at Jean.

"Yes, that's true; however, tax cuts are usually a conservative issue, and this Hale guy stole it from our platform!"

Still confused, Jean looks at Mitch.

"Why does it matter who presents the issue as long as it benefits the people?"

A bewildered Mitch looks at Jean.

"Because elections are not just about policy but also about the party. It's about strengthening our conservative base of power. Besides, if Hale keeps stealing our policies, we'll have nothing to run against him in the next election."

Jean enters the kitchen to prepare dinner. Since Mitch has an unpredictable work schedule, she typically eats before he arrives home. As she warms up his plate, she contemplates whether to share a job opportunity she found on social media.

After finishing with his plate, she slowly walks to the living room, hands him his dinner, and decides to go for it.

"Listen, Mitch, the last time we talked about me entering the workforce, I came into the living room and saw your dinner spread out on the floor."

Jean sits on the neighboring love seat as Mitch prays and starts eating his dinner.

"I think I found an answer to your concerns about me traveling to work by train."

Mitch watches Jean with a hint of curiosity as he eats his food.

"I can work from home and model for this new startup called Footlowfans."

Mitch turns his head, with food in his mouth, and begins to say something as Jean interrupts.

"And before you start thinking crazy, it's not some raunchy site. However, they're willing to pay a high commission to have me model their footwear. I think it's a fantastic deal! I don't have to leave my house. You don't have to worry about me traveling, and the best part is that I still get paid!"

Mitch knows he's in trouble because he's based his entire argument against Jean returning to work on his concerns about her traveling to Manhattan.

"I tell you what: Let me do some research, and I'll get back to you."

Jean smiles and kisses Mitch.

"Deal!"

She then grins and walks back to the kitchen.

As Mitch continues eating his dinner, he grabs his phone and frantically investigates the startup, mumbling to himself.

"With all the new startups happening because of this economic surge, I don't know where to begin."

As he eats and fumbles with his phone, Mitch continues his internet search.

Here it is!

The webpage's opening paragraph states: "*Footlowfans is a company that aims to showcase the greatest asset of the human body, its feet. We at Footlowfans have created an online platform dedicated to women and men who enjoy appreciating the human form, especially other people's footwear.*"

Mitch looks confused. *Other people's footwear? Oh ... I understand. This appears to be a shoe reseller or exchange website specializing in high-end shoes.*

Mitch scrolls down to read more.

"Footlowfans focuses on giving those with foot fetishes the chance to watch live videos of their favorite people's feet. Since our site provides total anonymity, providers can offer services securely without worrying about identity recognition for either side."

Mitch drops his fork. "Jean! Can you please come here for a second?"

Jean hurries into the living room. "Yes, Mitch?"

Mitch looks at Jean while holding his phone.

"I just found that new startup you mentioned and read their website's summary. Did you get a chance to browse the entire website?"

Filled with excitement, Jean responds.

"I just looked over the website and saw they were seeking potential models with attractive feet. I figured it would be a great way to earn money since I modeled shoes a few years ago. The best part is . . . you wouldn't have to worry about me traveling to work every day."

In exasperation, Mitch locks eyes with Jean, filled with disbelief.

"This company's not looking to sell shoes; they're looking to sell your feet."

Not understanding what Mitch is saying, she looks at him with concern.

"What do you mean?"

Mitch places his phone on the coffee table.

"I mean they're a website that caters to people who are attracted to other people's feet. You may not realize it, but people are willing to pay a lot of money to look at others' feet!"

Jean realizes what her husband is saying.

"Wow! I thought they were searching for people with nice feet to model their shoes."

Mitch picks up his phone from the coffee table and waves it at Jean.

"You see, you need to be cautious; these websites and apps can be misleading."

Jean grabs her phone from her pocket and starts scrolling for the website.

"So, how much do you think they pay?"

"What do you mean?"

Jean is still scrolling on her phone.

"How much do you think they would pay to see my feet?"

"Why do you care?"

Jean is now looking at the webpage on her phone.

"It says here that providers and their personal information are anonymous and protected. That's a good thing, right, Mitch?"

Mitch jumps up from the couch.

"Don't even think about it! No wife of mine is going to sell herself for money!"

Jean glares at Mitch with defiance.

"You stated that your issue with me working was the commute from Long Island to Manhattan. Well, I found a company willing to pay me a good amount just for showing others my feet. The best part is that my face won't be shown, and I have no tattoos, so there won't be any identity issues. How great is that?"

Mitch is furious and starts to pace the floor. "You're willing to sell yourself for a dollar!"

Jean lets out a light chuckle, amazed by Mitch's enraged response.

"Of course not. I'm willing to sell my feet for a dollar!"

"What happened to your Christian values?"

A frustrated Jean glares at Mitch.

"Hold on . . . Don't use religion as an excuse to make your point! Besides, where in the Bible does it say that what I consider acceptable is wrong? What's the difference between me modeling facial makeup and nightwear for everyone to see, or me modeling my feet for people? I'm not selling anything sexual, and I'm not defiling my body. I'm just showing my feet to an audience that would appreciate them. So, what's the problem?"

Mitch paces around the living room and points at Jean.

"This is crazy! You're my wife, and I forbid you from signing up with that site."

Jean stands face-to-face with Mitch.

"Forbid? Listen, I have only one heavenly father and one earthly father, and when either of them tells me to back down, I will. I have served you well over the past two decades, and you have faithfully provided for our daughters and me. However, the Bible notes that there's a time and place for everything, and at this moment, I will decide what is good for my life—not you!"

Jean storms out of the living room and heads back into the kitchen. Mitch now sits alone, wondering what just happened. Confused, he stands up from the couch, throws his hands in the air, and mutters to himself as he heads upstairs.

The mood at Paul's dinner table is lively with conversation and laughter. This is precisely what Paul had hoped for when he insisted that the family eat together. However, when the topic of education comes up, the mood shifts, casting a shadow over the otherwise joyful gathering.

"Preston, you're just about a year away from applying to college. Have you thought about what your majors might be?"

Preston and Pierce exchange glances and stay silent. After a moment, Paul looks at them and wonders if they heard him.

"Did you hear what I said? It may be helpful for both of you to consider careers at this stage in your life. Maybe one of you would even consider getting a degree in communications, just like I did."

Again, the boys nervously glance at each other and say nothing. Frustrated, Paul asks, "Hey! What's the problem?"

Kelly leans back in her chair, startled by Paul's tone. "Paul, relax! Why are you getting so upset?"

Paul fixates his eyes on Kelly, wondering if she has absorbed what just happened.

"These boys heard me talking to them and intentionally ignored me."

Pierce reluctantly jumps in and speaks up in a low voice. "Dad, we're considering not going to college."

Paul, not sure of what he heard, turns to Pierce. "What did you say?"

Pierce nervously looks at Preston. "You tell him!"

Preston stops eating and looks at his father. "Dad, we're considering not going to college."

Paul places his fork down and looks at Kelly. "Kelly, do you hear this?"

Kelly nods her head but says nothing.

Paul turns to his sons.

"So, you guys can sneak around, smoke weed in my home, and think that's okay. Yet, when it comes to education . . ."

Frustrated, Paul stops speaking. Kelly leans in.

"Paul, let the boys speak. It's their lives!"

Paul looks at Pierce.

"Okay, okay . . . What are your plans?"

Preston and Pierce exchange a look.

"We're looking into being professional gamers."

Paul drops his fork, causing food to splatter across the table. "Excuse me?"

"We're looking to make money playing video games."

Confused, Paul turns to Kelly. "Is this a joke? Did you know about this? When did this mindset develop, and why was I not notified?"

Kelly shrugs and says nothing as he turns his attention back to his sons.

"As a talk show host, I've heard of everything, but I've never heard of a professional gamer. Do they make money, and if so, how much?"

Preston and Pierce have no clear answers, so they shift the topic back to their father.

"Listen, Dad, you said that we should be happy with the career we choose. You said that if our job is something we love, we would never work a day in our lives. So, we chose what makes us happy . . . video games."

Paul drops his face into his hands and shakes his head.

"I did say that; however, you need to experience more of life to get a fuller picture of what the world offers. President Hale opened the floodgates of education, providing anyone who wanted to attend college a voucher and interest-free loans to help cover tuition at any school in the country. It's a major investment this nation is making in its youth, and I expected you to take advantage of it!"

No one says anything as they keep eating. Preston and Pierce show no interest in Paul's words. However, the night is still young, and Paul refuses to give up.

"Why don't you guys consider attending a community college for two years to get a feel for the atmosphere, campus life, and course options? It's a short-term commitment that can help you decide if college is the right choice."

Pierce looks at his father. "Does community college have courses in gaming?"

Paul looks at his son in disbelief and hollers, "Are you for real?"

Kelly nervously jumps in. "Paul! Please lower your voice."

Paul looks at Kelly, then looks at Pierce.

"All right, sorry, Pierce. To answer your question, colleges probably don't offer gaming courses. However, they do have courses in computer science and AI technology that can help you understand the gaming world."

Preston says, "No, Dad, we're only interested in gaming. Not all that other stuff you're talking about."

What started as a pleasant dinner turned into a painful night for Paul.

"Listen, boys, even if you love your work, please understand it might not support the lifestyle you want, including maintaining the comfortable standard of living you currently enjoy. Do you understand what I am saying?"

Preston and Pierce just sit there, staring at their father. Overcome with frustration, Paul suddenly rises from the dinner table, mutters to himself, and steps out onto his balcony for some fresh air.

Meanwhile, a startled Kelly and the boys stay at the table, quiet, wondering how the evening had suddenly shifted. Breaking the silence, Preston looks at his mother with a slight smile on his face.

"Well, I guess that ends the experiment of us eating dinner together."

Stunned by her son's carefree attitude about what just happened, Kelly looks at Preston and uncharacteristically shouts, "If you and your brother are not at this table tomorrow night for dinner, you're grounded for life!"

Amid the chatter of Kelly and the boys talking in the kitchen, Paul stands on the balcony, confused, wondering why his own success, which had affected millions of listeners nationwide, hasn't seemed to influence his sons.

As the city settles into the night, Tony finishes his podcast, puts on his jacket, and heads to Nicole's house. He enjoys sharing meals and having stimulating conversations with her a few times a week. When he arrives and rings the doorbell, Jason unexpectedly opens the door, still wearing his pajamas from that morning.

"Hey, Mr. Stravell, how are you doing?"

Tony looks disappointed as he stares at Jason.

"I'm doing all right. What got you out of the basement this evening?"

Jason laughs.

"My mother's cooking . . . Come on in."

Jason lets Tony in and walks with him into the living room.

Typically, when Tony visits, Jason is often absent. It's usually Nicole who pulls him from the basement to come upstairs and greet Tony. As Tony takes off his coat, Jason turns and shouts from the living room:

"Mom, Mr. Stravell is here!"

Nicole's faint voice comes from the kitchen. "Thanks, Jason, I will be out in a moment."

Tony sits down on the couch, and Jason joins him while they wait for dinner to be served. Aware of how sensitive Nicole is to her son, Tony tries to stay calm as he talks with Jason.

"So, Jason, since the last time we spoke, what has been going on in your life?"

Jason smiles.

"Well, I have been doing my best to find myself and figure out what my future holds."

Tony nods his head up and down. "You're almost thirty years old and have a degree in communications. How much longer do you need to look for yourself?"

Jason laughs.

"Come on, Mr. Stravell. We've talked about this before. For me to be happy, I need to find a job that meets my needs, excites my senses, and fulfills my desires."

Tony has a confused look on his face.

"Are you talking about getting a job or having sex?"

Jason laughs.

"Mr. Stravell, if I must work somewhere for eight hours, I should be comfortable."

Tony knows this conversation is going nowhere; however, he continues anyway.

"I sent you numerous job opportunities you could have applied for, including one working with me part-time at the studio."

Jason looks at Tony. "I hear you, but that position was not willing to pay me what I'm worth."

Frustrated, Tony continues. "But you haven't held a job since you graduated. Your life revolves around social media and playing video games in the basement; yet you're trying to convince me of your worth?"

Jason quickly replies, "Yes, I'm worth it because there's so much more to me than a piece of paper stating I graduated."

"My offer then and now is for you to work with me. This would give you a foot in the door and help you network your way to a full-time position."

Jason looks at Tony.

"Mr. Stravell, thank you, but I think you're doing too much! I've found a better option than working a nine-to-five job. I plan to become a social media influencer, using my creativity to earn a living and bring happiness to others. Even better, I don't have to clock in or out, and I can set my own hours. Neither you nor my mom understands that I need to feel comfortable!"

"Well, how is that working out for you now? You're in the basement of your mother's home with no job, no medical insurance, and no driver's license—"

Jason, unconcerned, interrupts. "Maybe that's true, but I don't need a lot of money to be happy. My happiness doesn't depend on buying a house, driving an expensive car, or taking luxury vacations. That's something your generation needs to feel important and impress others. I have nothing to prove to anyone. I don't need someone else's name on my shirts, a brand on my shoes, or a fancy car to boost my self-esteem. I'm happy living a minimalist life, and if that means living with my mom for the rest of my life, so be it!"

Tony stares at him in disbelief, struggling to comprehend what he's just heard. He feels a strong urge to challenge Jason's apparent ignorance and arrogance. However, just as Tony is prepared to unleash his thoughts, Nicole steps out of the kitchen.

"Dinner is ready!"

And just like that, the conversation is over.

11

Tricky Choices

President Hale enters his second year in office and is confident that his initiatives will strengthen the economy. However, like any politician aiming to secure their position, he is already planning to run for reelection, hoping it will help him reach his goals.

As he sits in his office, President Hale calls his adviser for a briefing. Mr. Bishop already knows what the president needs and brings his laptop, ready to answer any questions.

"Mr. Bishop, give me an update on the current economy and our projections for the rest of my term."

As Mr. Bishop scrolls through his laptop, the president adds, "Just to clarify, I need to know what's expected by the start of the next election cycle."

Mr. Bishop nods as he continues to scroll for the data.

"Here it is, Mr. President. Are you looking for something specific, or would you prefer a general overview?"

The president pauses for a moment.

"I want an overall projection of our five-point policy for the next two years."

Mr. Bishop nods in approval.

"Okay, Mr. President."

Mr. Bishop begins briefing the president on the economic projections prepared by his economists and staff regarding the nation's future. He highlights the robust condition of the economy and the expected growth over the next two years. He notes that more lower and middle-class families will have young adults enrolled in secondary education during his presidency than at any other time in this nation's history.

As the president smiles, Mr. Bishop continues. "Mr. President, by the time of the next election, every citizen will have access to medical care during your presidency, more than ever before in the country's history. Additionally, thanks to the funding you have provided, the nation will improve its military capabilities with advanced technology, thereby strengthening its ability to defend against all enemies."

Mr. Bishop looks at the president, who forces a smile.

"Finally, Mr. President, your family values policy has set a precedent for promoting respect for other people's choices. You acknowledged the government can influence opinions but cannot change hearts. This key point highlighted the delicate balance between the government's role and personal beliefs. I believe this showed you as an intellectual and will boost your chances for reelection."

The president nods, listens carefully, and thinks a moment as Mr. Bishop closes his laptop and looks up.

"All right, Mr. Bishop, great presentation. Thanks for the update. If there are any changes to these projections, please let me know immediately."

Mr. Bishop smiles, stands up, and walks toward the door. "Yes, sir, Mr. President."

As he opens the door, Mr. Bishop turns around and looks at the president.

"Mr. President, what steps will you take to fight global warming? There's a small but passionate group advocating for actions to lessen its effect."

The president pauses before looking at Mr. Bishop, who is holding the door open.

"I avoided that topic during my campaign for reasons you already know. There's a lot of activity happening out there, and our goal is to do what we can to protect this existing structure. That's why we're here. Right now, it's not in our best interest to address that issue. But I promise we'll handle it when the time comes."

Mr. Bishop gazes intently and nods at the President as he walks out the door.

"Yes, sir. Thank you, sir."

At Mitch's house, his relationship with Jean appears to be falling apart. He steps outside to gather some packages. Since Jean started working at Footlowfans, their relationship has changed significantly. Looking back, Mitch wishes they hadn't allowed their disagreements to escalate so much.

As Mitch walks upstairs to tell Jean about her delivery, he opens the door to their room and finds her sitting on the bed, massaging her legs and feet.

"Jean, you have a couple of packages downstairs."

"Okay, thank you."

Mitch sits in a chair across from the bed.

"You know, it's been a year since you asked about being a foot model, and honestly, I initially thought you were joking about actually doing it."

Jean looks at Mitch as she finishes massaging one of her legs.

"Well, you complained about me working in the city, making me feel torn between my desires and your expectations. So, instead of arguing with you, I decided to pray about it, hoping God would give me insight."

Mitch's eyes widen, and her words take him aback. "Really? You prayed about this?"

Jean smirks. "Yes, I did. Is that surprising to you?"

"So, you prayed about your new job, showing your feet to strangers, and He approved?"

"I'm not claiming He said yes, but I'm also not asserting He said no. So, I'll keep doing what I do until I hear otherwise."

Mitch stands up.

"So, morally, are you comfortable with your role as an internet foot model, wiggling your toes for strangers?"

Jean switches to her other leg and massages it.

"I'm comfortable earning my own money, and I like not hearing you complain about my ability to take care of myself.

Besides, the economy is booming, and there's money to be made!"

Jean smiles as Mitch shakes his head in disbelief.

"Jean, do you have any spiritual convictions about what you're doing or how it affects our relationship or my job?"

Jean becomes serious as she replies.

"First, how could my choice hurt your career? No one can see my face. I don't have tattoos or birthmarks that are identifiable, and I'm safe in my own home. Isn't this what you wanted?"

Mitch stays quiet.

"Until God tells me otherwise, I plan to get a pedicure each week, soak my feet, and have my legs massaged for my clients."

Mitch's eyes opened wide.

"Clients? That sounds like you're selling something else! You didn't tell me you have clients! I thought this was just a look-and-see group thing."

Jean smiles, grabs some lotion, and starts moisturizing her legs.

"Sometimes people prefer not to be in a group setting and might ask for personal time."

Mitch scratches his head and stares at Jean, attempting to comprehend what he is hearing.

"You're getting a kick out of throwing this in my face, aren't you?"

Mitch walks toward the door and reaches into his pocket. Realizing he doesn't have his cell phone, he grabs Jean's phone from the dresser.

"I'm going to use your phone to try to locate my phone."

Jean nervously watches Mitch try to unlock her phone. After three failed attempts, he pauses. "Why can't I unlock it? It won't let me in."

Jeans slowly looks up from massaging her leg and mumbles, "I changed the password."

Mitch places the phone back on the dresser.

"I don't think I heard you correctly. You did what?"

Jean slowly glances at Mitch and speaks louder. "I said I changed the password."

Stunned, Mitch stares at Jean and sits down.

"You changed the password to your phone to stop me from accessing it. After over twenty years of marriage, during which we have intentionally shared our passwords to show transparency, you chose to lock me out of your phone—and your life!"

Jean says nothing as she sits on her bed, rolls her eyes, and listens as Mitch vents.

"Since the day we got married, we agreed that there would be no secrets between us. We reaffirmed this commitment by being transparent and sharing our cell phone passcodes. In fact, we even created a joint marriage email account so that all communication regarding our household or our children could be sent there, ensuring that both of us stay informed in real time."

Jean, knowing everything Mitch is saying is true, says nothing.

"But now, you have compromised any trust left in this marriage by hiding things from me!"

Before Mitch can say another word, Jean interjects.

"Look, Mitch, I'm not doing anything I believe compromises our marriage."

Mitch shouts. "You changed your password on your phone!"

Jean's face shows remorse as she tries to explain herself.

"Yes, I did, but the only reason I did that was to protect us."

Flustered and confused, Mitch stands up.

"Protect us from what!"

Jean, hearing Mitch's tone, calmly says, "I wanted to protect you from misunderstanding the text messages that come in about my work."

Confusion flows across Mitch's face. "What?"

"Look, when I accepted the job as a foot model, I did so knowing that my personal interactions and details about my life would stay private and discreet, and they have. However, there are times when the manager might contact us to check on our clients and ensure that our interactions comply with the rules and are safe. I realized that seeing these kinds of messages could make you uncomfortable. So, to protect you and our marriage, I decided to secure my phone."

Mitch stares back at her as silence fills the air. Then he says, "Nice try, but that sounds like nonsense! You applied for this position in secret, without my knowledge, locked yourself in the guest room for privacy, restricted my access to your phone, and kept showing your feet to strangers. I really don't want to hear any more of your lies and freaky stuff! I'm going downstairs!"

As he walks to the door, Jean shouts, "You don't complain about that freaky stuff when we're together—and you're sucking my toes!"

Mitch looks at Jean, smirks, shakes his head in disapproval, and goes downstairs. Frustrated and feeling like she needs to say something else, Jean yells, "Don't worry, Mitch. You won't lose out! There are enough toes for everyone!"

"Oh! It's like that!" Mitch yells back. "You don't need to worry about me being part of that group anymore!"

As Jean sits on the bed, she mumbles to herself, "God, I probably should not have said that."

Nevertheless, she puts on her dress and carefully chooses the perfect high heels for her client. Then, she goes to the guest room to prepare for her first appointment of the day and locks the door behind her. As she sets up her camera and adjusts the lighting, her heart races with nervousness, wondering whether her client will be pleased. She knows that making a good first impression is crucial in determining how the rest of the session unfolds.

As Jean finishes her last adjustments, the camera's timer starts its countdown to the live stream.

Five, four, three, two, one . . . Recording.

Paul faces a different kind of tension. He still finds it hard to accept his sons' decision to pursue careers in video games. Once again, what is supposed to be a friendly family dinner turns into a discussion that clears the table.

"All right, family, I know it's been a while since we got together because of my busy schedule."

His sons share a look and smile.

"I understand that you boys are interested in gaming, and I'm willing to support your choices; however, I want you to explore other areas of technology to broaden your skills. Since you're not planning to attend college, I have a friend who works in the government. His name is Mr. Sinclair. He's researching practical applications of artificial intelligence in science and technology, and I would like you to intern with him when the program opens up."

Preston looks at Pierce, then looks at his father.

"Dad, I don't know why you're doing this. Gamers can't use artificial intelligence in competition."

Paul's face shows an expression of exasperation as he glares at Preston.

"I don't know if gamers use AI or not, but I do know that you guys need a more balanced understanding of technology if you want to get ahead."

Preston and Pierce roll their eyes as Paul continues.

"Listen, AI is the future, and this summer program will broaden your understanding of its applications. I encourage you both to participate."

Preston stares at his father, stunned and struggling to understand what he's heard.

"Hey, Dad, we already know what we want to do for a living. We want to be professional gamers."

Paul raises his voice.

"How many times are you going to tell me that? Until the gaming community provides a place for you to live, you must do this internship. Do you understand?"

The boys keep eating their dinner as if Paul hadn't asked them a question. When he realizes he's being ignored, Paul yells, "I said, do you hear me!"

Kelly, startled by Paul's tone, moves to calm things down.

"Please, Paul, relax. The boys are just trying to figure out where they're going and what they want to do in life."

Preston, not realizing that his mother is trying to support their choices, says, "No, Mom, we made up our minds, and we're going to be gamers."

Kelly narrows her eyes at Preston as she continues to emphasize her point.

"Sweetheart, I admire your dedication and determination; however, you should consider keeping all options open."

Feeling frustrated, Paul reenters the conversation.

"All right. Regardless, I'll be signing both of you boys up for the program."

Preston mumbles, "It would be just a waste of time."

Paul hears him but says, "Excuse me, what did you say?"

Sitting next to Preston and fearing another outburst, Pierce jumps in. "He said nothing, Dad."

Paul glares at Preston, lowers his tone, and tries to reason with his sons.

"Boys, this summer internship could not only improve your understanding of the gaming world but also help you embrace technology overall. I don't know much about the gaming industry, but is it possible that understanding the technology behind the gaming platform could improve your gaming skills?"

Preston and Pierce exchange glances, think for a moment, and say nothing as they keep eating their dinner. Paul, feeling ignored and somewhat disrespected again, says, "Oh, so now you guys have nothing to say."

Again, both boys keep eating.

"All right, that's enough! Preston and Pierce, put down your food and go to your rooms! Forget television, video games, internet browsing, or any form of entertainment until you learn some respect."

Pierce stares at his father in confusion.

"But Dad, we didn't say anything."

Paul glares back at his younger son.

"That's the problem!"

Pierce feels confused as he and his brother stand up and push their chairs back from the dinner table. Still hungry, they grab the remaining pieces of chicken from the table with their hands, along with some bread and fries. Food falls all over the floor as they run down the hallway to their rooms.

Stunned, Paul looks at Kelly while rubbing his head in frustration.

"Did you see what I just saw? What kind of cavemen do we have for sons? I read somewhere that most families today no longer sit down to dinner together. Now tell me, what is the mindset for anyone to push back against a family eating together?"

Kelly does not say a word but notices that Paul is taking his son's choices personally. Seeing him struggling to understand, she says, "Listen, you're a good father who has done everything possible to educate, provide for, and protect our family. Ultimately, the boys will need to learn how to navigate life's challenges on their own and live with the consequences of their choices."

Paul lovingly looks at Kelly.

"Thank you, sweetheart. Sometimes the encourager needs encouragement."

Tony is finishing up his podcast for the night and is looking forward to dinner at Nicole's house.

"Podcast family, I mentioned earlier in my show that our nation is experiencing unusual economic growth. However, I also emphasized the importance of looking beyond the surface to uncover the truth. The superficial politics practiced by both sides of the aisle, including this Independent president, can hide what is buried only for so long. While the projected economic numbers for this year seem to be stable, a closer look at next year's forecasts indicates that a major correction is coming."

Tony begins clearing his desk and packing his bags as he continues.

"Okay, family, I must head out. This is Tony Stravell on *The Gray Forum*. Please support my podcast, and remember, what you see on the surface is meant for you to see. I'll see you tomorrow. Have a good night."

As Tony waves to Rob, he rushes to his car and calls Nicole. "Nicole, sweetheart, I'm running a little late. How are you doing?"

It is the night of the week when Nicole and Tony get together at her house for dinner.

"Hey, Tony, I'm doing great. How are you feeling?"

Tony is backing out of his parking space and heads toward Eleventh Avenue.

"I'm feeling good because in a few minutes, I'm going to see my baby and enjoy dinner!"

Nicole laughs.

"I can't wait to see you, too. Listen, I'm getting off this phone to finish cooking. I'll see you in a few."

Tony makes a left on Eleventh Ave and heads uptown. "No problem, sweetheart. See you soon."

Tony turns off his phone's speaker mode and drives east toward Second Avenue. About thirty minutes later, he arrives at Nicole's house. Most of the time, Tony and Nicole eat alone while Jason stays in the basement, immersed in social media and video games.

Despite his mother's warnings, he rarely goes upstairs to say hello or goodbye. But for Tony, that is perfectly fine because he knows he and Nicole would have the chance to watch a movie and enjoy some private time together.

At the door, Tony grabs his cell phone, switches the camera angle to check himself out, then rings the doorbell. Jason answers.

"What the hell!"

Jason smiles.

"Surprised to see me, huh?"

Tony shakes his head in disbelief as he stares at Jason.

"*Surprised* is not the word. What are you doing answering the door?"

Jason looks at Tony.

"What do you mean, Mr. Stravell? Can't a man answer the door in his own home?"

Tony is tempted to tell Jason he has no home, but he resists.

"Well, are you just going to let me stand out here, or are you going to let me in?"

Jason steps back.

"Oh, sorry, Mr. Stravell, come in."

This is only the second time in two years that Jason has greeted Tony at the door. The first time they met, they'd argued until Nicole came out with dinner. Now, they find themselves in a similar situation, waiting for dinner to arrive. Neither of them wants to start a conversation, fearing it might cause controversy. However, since Jason is in the living room, Tony decides to break the ice.

"Hey, Jason, I have a question for you. In all the years I've been dating your mother, you've never come up from the basement to say hi. Why did you come out to greet me twice in the last two years?"

Jason smiles.

"Mr. Stravell, my being up here has nothing to do with you. It just happens that on the two occasions you visited, my mother prepared my favorite dish. To encourage her to keep cooking for me, I show her my appreciation by coming upstairs."

Tony shakes his head in disappointment as Jason continues.

"In other words, Mr. Stravell, your presence has nothing to do with why I'm upstairs."

Tony looks at Jason and sarcastically replies, "Wow! Thanks for letting me know."

While both men wait patiently for dinner, Jason decides to open up to Tony.

"Mr. Stravell, I know we don't speak too often; however, our last conversation made me think."

Tony rolls his eyes. *Oh, boy. This is going to be good.*

"About three years ago, I stopped at a bar on my way home and met a guy who was playing pool with his friends. We started talking, and I learned that he owned a social media advertising firm. After chatting with him between pool shots, we both agreed that life is too short to work in a job that doesn't make you feel competent and appreciated."

Tony is listening carefully, trying to follow the story.

"Mr. Stravell, this guy understood where I was coming from when I said I wanted a career working in social media, influencing people and making them happy. He stated that he operates a business collaborating with several Fortune 500 companies, universities, colleges, and even presidents to develop social media platforms that engage, inform, and gather data critical for their clients."

Tony nods his head, impressed.

"You know, Jason, that sounds good, but some of these guys are full of it. Did he tell you which companies and corporations he worked for? Even better, let's check to see which college and university presidents he's worked with."

Jason has a confused look on his face.

"Mr. Stravell, he was not talking about college and university presidents; he was talking about the social media platform he created for President Hale."

Tony sits up on the sofa, astounded.

"You mean the leader of this nation, President Hale?"

Jason replies, "Yes, sir. He claims his social media ads played a key role in getting the president elected and showed me a picture of himself and the president looking at a computer monitor. Here, take a look. I took a picture of it with my cell phone."

Tony stares at the picture in disbelief, realizing that the social media campaign created by this young man and his organization has played a key role in helping the president get elected. Tony hasn't seen President Hale since he interviewed him during the campaign three years ago, and now Jason has a real chance to work for a respected organization that backed his campaign.

With more to the story, Jason continues.

"After talking with him, he sat down and asked for my opinion on his organization. I told him that I believe his company is a great platform for promoting meaningful issues on social media, and I'm interested in learning more about what his agency does."

Jason's expression reflects a mix of enthusiasm and caution.

"Mr. Stravell, this brother reached into his pocket and gave me his business card, along with his social media contacts. He told me to contact him. He said that because of the economic boom, business is great, and he could use some help on his team with corporate clients and the president's reelection campaign."

Tony smiles in amazement. "So, what happened after that?"

"You know, Mr. Stravell, I'm not exactly sure what happened. I took his business card and then went to the restroom. When I came out, I saw him in a heated argument with a large White guy about politics. As the discussion escalated, people gathered around, and things seemed to be getting out of control. I stood by the bar, watching from a distance, but when I saw his friends get up and surround the White guy, I decided not to stay and left."

Tony is somewhat curious. "Wow! So, why and how did you decide to contact this guy years later?"

Jason smiles. "My last conversation with you made me reflect on my perspective and question whether I'd been a little too narrow-minded in my thinking. While I still need to find a job that makes me happy, maybe for now, I should explore other options."

Tony has a slight smile on his face, while Jason continues.

"Last week, while cleaning my gaming desk, I found his business card and decided to call him."

Tony looks at Jason in anticipation. "So, what happened?"

"He didn't remember me until I reminded him where we'd met, specifically mentioning the incident in the bar with the White guy. He said he would need assistance with some new contracts headed his way and would call me when they came through."

Tony has a massive smile on his face, knowing this could be Jason's chance to get out and find his own place.

"Listen, Jason, if there's anything I can do to help you succeed in getting this position, please let me know."

Jason nods his head but looks skeptical. "What's with the big smile on your face?"

Not wanting to express his true feelings, Tony glances around the room for a distraction and then sees Nicole emerge from the kitchen.

"Why wouldn't I smile? It's dinnertime!"

12

Ripple Effect

Now in his third year in office, President Hale faces several challenges related to his ambitious five-point plan. Economists predict a slowdown primarily driven by increased spending, rising demand, and a lack of supplies, all contributing to inflation. Unfortunately, these economic forecasts overshadow Hale's initiatives, forcing him to address unexpected fiscal challenges.

Amid economic worries, the president sits at his desk, concerned about the progress of his five-point plan. He knows that if the first part fails, it could trigger a ripple effect that threatens the success of his entire policy agenda. Feeling anxious, he calls in his adviser to discuss the state of the economy and his future.

Mr. Bishop walks into the room and routinely shakes the president's hand. "Greetings, Mr. President."

The president nods and gets right to the point. "Mr. Bishop, have a seat."

Mr. Bishop sits in a chair directly across from the president's desk.

"Over the past few years, we have fulfilled all five promises made to the people, and everything we aimed to accomplish is on track. However, we're at risk of facing a fiscal problem at best and an economic crisis at worst. The people haven't yet felt the full impact of what is financially projected, but if they do, they will look for someone to blame, and that person cannot be me!"

Mr. Bishop listens intently, then chimes in. "Mr. President, the five-point plan was successful. We've held this office for three years, and I'm confident that we will defeat any opponent in the upcoming campaign. However, no one expected that our tax plan would be so effective that the public would go on a spending spree, driving up prices and placing an unreasonable strain on suppliers worldwide."

The president nods and smiles as Mr. Bishop continues.

"I know you may not want to hear this, but hear me out. What if we pushed for a budget bill that gradually raises taxes? This could help ease our economic challenges and generate extra funds."

The president is not happy with his adviser's suggestion.

"That, sir, is not an option! We're headed toward an election year, and the legislative process would take too long to complete. We must find a quick solution to this fiscal problem to maintain the integrity of my five-point plan."

Mr. Bishop looks curiously at the president.

"What do you mean when you say you need a quick solution?"

President Hale slides his chair back and stands up.

"I mean, we need to provide quick fixes to long-term problems to secure my reelection and complete our purpose. Once the election is over, we can think long-term. However, I'm telling you now, if the solution requires raising taxes, then leave me out of it!"

Mr. Bishop notices the intense expression on the president's face.

"I understand, Mr. President. I want to suggest a strategy that could strengthen your campaign."

The President locks his eyes on Mr. Bishop and crosses his arms across his chest.

"Okay, Mr. Bishop, let me hear it."

Mr. Bishop stands up and walks toward the president.

"Research is currently ongoing to examine how artificial intelligence can be utilized across all agencies to boost productivity and increase efficiency. A key benefit of AI is its capacity to process data and generate simulations, enabling us to forecast future outcomes. For example, we might employ AI to analyze the economic data we receive in our daily briefings and conduct simulations to project what the fiscal year could look like before the election. This strategy would give you a strategic edge over your political rivals and those opposing your agenda in Congress."

The president smiles and walks toward the Presidential Office window. "Now, that sounds interesting. When can we get this thing going?"

Mr. Bishop grabs his briefcase.

"I'll contact Mr. Sinclair, the head of our research department, to inform him of our request. He's currently working on several high-priority AI projects, including cybersecurity, environmental solutions, and space exploration."

The president firmly rests his hand on Mr. Bishop's shoulder as they walk to the door.

"Well, Mr. Bishop, I didn't realize how clever you are. All this time, you've been devising a strategy that could effectively support our mission, such as contacting Mr. Sinclair."

Mr. Bishop looks at the president.

"Thank you, Mr. President, for listening. It's my job to keep you focused on your purpose. I'll follow up on our discussion as soon as I can. Have a good day."

As predicted, the nation's financial situation continues to weaken, and reports indicate that the public is beginning to accept that these developments could adversely affect their standard of living. What is even more troubling is the risk of panic, similar to what occurred during the COVID-19 pandemic.

Inside his studio, Mitch is about to start his show.

"Welcome to the one and only *Consultant of Conservatism* on WCONS in New York City. All right, let's skip the formalities and get right to the point."

Mitch leans forward and adjusts his microphone.

"Ladies and gentlemen, I warned you. I warned you that President Hale's promises were unrealistic. I pointed out that although he had a general outline of his policies, he lacked a clear understanding of what it truly takes to run a nation. He told you what you wanted to hear and simplified his message so much that you accepted it without question, like a baby drinking its mother's milk. He knew that the population could not handle the truth, and to paraphrase a great civil rights activist, it looks like the chickens have come home to roost."

Mitch grabs his coffee from his desk and sips it.

"Family, I know you appreciated hearing a straightforward five-point plan that was easy to understand and support. Heck, even my wife thought the five-point plan was clever, and to be transparent, I won't deny that we conservatives should perhaps simplify our policy approach. However, the issue with Hale's policy is that he proposed it through a narrow lens. He did not realize that multiple layers of subpolicies contribute to the overall policy's success. His administration has overlooked essential economic indicators vital to maintaining the nation's stability. It's an amateur oversight, made by an amateur politician who created a flawed amateur policy!"

Mitch looks at Jake as he continues.

"Just three months into the year, inflation is expected to rise to levels not seen since 1981. The situation is so uncertain that even the National Monetary Reserve is hesitant to act until a clearer economic picture emerges. Now, it appears everything is falling apart, and the president is at risk of losing reelection."

Mitch leaned back in his chair as Jake notified him that it's time for a break.

"Ladies and gentlemen, I have been doing this for a long time, and with my insight and brilliance, I believe I have figured out Hale's strategy. He believed that by not raising taxes, Congress would do his dirty work and quickly pass an emergency bill to increase taxes. However, he appears to have forgotten how he forced Congress to pass his five-point plan. Now, my sources inform me that Congress does not care about Hale's chances of reelection, and if the national economy falters under his administration, so be it!"

Mitch laughs as he prepares to go to the restroom.

"As the saying goes, Mr. Hale, payback is a bitch! We'll be right back after these words from our sponsors."

In all his years of broadcasting experience, Paul has never seen such a rapid economic decline. He's gained recognition for being progressive and for holding politicians accountable to their constituents. He takes a blunt approach toward conservatives, believing their policies contribute to the nation's problems.

Now, with the country led by its first Independent president, Paul is not holding back on criticizing a failing tax policy that threatens working-class families.

As he waits in his studio for Rochelle to give him the ready sign, he pulls his chair up to his desk, full of energy and ready to go.

"America! Welcome to WPROG in New York City, home of the number one nationally syndicated liberal talk show host in the nation. Our politics are simple. We're open-minded, freethinking, generous Americans who love our country and wish to see the rights of all Americans upheld."

Paul takes off his jacket as he continues.

"America, what are we going to do about President Hale? It has been three years, and you would think there would be a backup plan in case things did not go his way. You cannot significantly cut taxes and increase spending without recognizing that programs will be negatively impacted."

Paul leans back in his chair.

"I want to ask my audience a question: If this fiscal correction happens, what will it mean for national health care coverage? What effect will it have on educational support for the millions of students aiming to do more than their parents?"

Paul pauses and sips his coffee.

"It's interesting to observe that without education, a family starting in poverty is likely to remain in poverty unless there's a major change in their situation. Although I'm not a supporter of President Hale, I must recognize that his second policy on education and his third policy on health care are initiatives I support."

Rochelle waves her hand for a break.

"The president started his campaign strong, but it seems his policies are weakening as another election approaches. If he loses, he will face a harsh truth about himself: His five-point policy was just a house of cards, built on a shaky foundation and ready to fall."

Paul looks up at Rochelle and gives her a thumbs-up.

"We'll be right back after a word from our sponsors."

While Mitch and Paul remain frustrated with President Hale, Tony is at his desk, preparing to start another episode of *The Gray Forum*.

"Good afternoon, Gray Forum family! While I was driving to work today, I listened to talk radio. Both Republican and Democratic commentators expressed concerns about the economy's future. Overall, their outlook on the predicted decline of our economic system was quite disturbing."

Tony flicks through his notes as he continues.

"However, Mitch Corvane said something today that I completely agree with. He stated that the issue with Hale's policy is that it was proposed through a narrow lens. He did not understand that multiple layers of subpolicies contribute to the success of an overall policy."

Tony slams his papers on his desk.

"You see, that's exactly what I've been talking about all these years! Mitch was right: Multiple layers of subpolicies shape a politician's agenda, and my role, as well as the goal of this podcast, is to look beneath the surface and decode them. I call this process top-layer politics. For those new to my program, top-layer politics means the spread of hyperpolitical talking points that look like oil on water's surface, hiding everything underneath."

Tony maintains a serious expression as he continues speaking.

"The saying *the devil is in the details* highlights the importance of uncovering the truth that often lies beneath the surface. President Hale's campaign seems to be close to panic, with economic indicators pointing to a slowdown just before the election."

Tony pauses and sips some of his water.

"When I interviewed then-candidate Hale three years ago, he was confident that his five-point plan would help him win the presidency, and he was right. However, as time passed, it became evident that his policies were vague and primarily intended to resonate with the public's emotions.

Tony looks up from his notes at Rob, who gives him a thumbs-up.

"For decades, we have been misled by a two-party system that pretends to act independently but collaborates on many policies. Today, I heard about both parties in Congress uniting to oppose President Hale. They were content during the first three years when the money was flowing, and their constituents were spending freely. However, when the economy slowed, they refused to develop a policy to help the president. Instead, they came together and plotted revenge on the president for pressuring them when he won the election."

Tony bangs his fist on his chair as he finishes his monologue.

"But what do you expect? They are politicians. When things get tough, some of them will throw you under the bus. Now, I'm not saying that President Hale doesn't deserve criticism for his policies; however, we still have months left until the election. Let's see how his administration handles adversity and the media for the first time."

Rob held up the sign for a break.

"This is Tony Stravell on *The Gray Forum*. Remember: What you see on the surface is meant for you to see. We'll be right back after a word from our sponsors."

13

Controlled Impact

Good evening. This is a special report from the National News Center in New York. In a remarkable development, the economy is now experiencing an unexpected period of inflation. As prices rise for essentials such as milk, eggs, cheese, and paper products, economists note that middle-class disposable incomes are shrinking. Additionally, the National News Center has received data indicating that sales of goods and services have declined substantially, which could lead to nationwide layoffs. National News Center will continue to keep you updated on this rapidly changing economic situation as we approach the election season. This has been a special report. We now return you to your regularly scheduled programming."

Jean has been listening to the radio in the bedroom.

"Mitch! Mitch! Did you hear the news report?"

Mitch comes out of the bathroom, drying his hands, and heads toward the living room as Jean catches up to him.

"No, Jean, I was in the bathroom."

Jean rolls her eyes as she continues.

"This is crazy. Three years ago, the economy looked promising. People were spending generously, and I was earning a good income, showing my ..."

Mitch listens as Jean suddenly stops, pausing midsentence.

"I mean, everyone was making good money, but now, the news reports that we're facing serious economic issues and hints at a possible recession."

Mitch looks at Jean as she follows him into the living room.

"It sounds like you're worried about your career as a so-called foot model. You know what? I'm curious about how this economic crisis affects your clients and whether it causes them to stop using your services. As a result, would you raise your prices to cover the loss of clients, or lower your prices to attract new ones?"

As Jean thinks about the question, Mitch smirks as he sits down and picks up the remote.

"That, Jean, is an example of the decisions this nation has to face because of this president and his advisers."

Mitch, looking frustrated, stares at Jean as he turns on the TV.

"Let me say this: I have dealt with your foot modeling and toe-peeping career long enough! I'm tired of your job and of you waiting for God to give you an answer as to whether you should continue as a foot model."

Jean, looking confused, walks closer to Mitch, sitting on a white leather couch in the center of the living room. "Where is your patience and understanding?"

Mitch gazes curiously at Jean, wondering what thoughts are running through her mind.

"I have been waiting three years for God to tell you that you're wrong. Could it be that He doesn't need to tell you because you already know it's problematic? Even worse, is it possible that your drive to be independent is overriding your ability to hear Him speak?"

Jeans says nothing as Mitch continues to get his feelings off his chest.

"Listen, I need you to understand that I can't handle this foot situation anymore. You're my wife, and you represent the Corvane family. I can't risk someone finding out what you're doing and using it against me!"

Jean glares at Mitch in disbelief. "Using it against you, how?"

Mitch browses through the channels on the eighty-inch flat-screen TV.

"I don't know, but I do know that God knows that I'm not happy, and something has to change."

Jean walks over and stands between Mitch and the TV.

"Well, Mitch, what about my happiness? For the first time in my life, I have a choice about what I want to do. I now have my own checking account, something I've never had before, and I can make purchases without logging into our joint account. How can you have issues with a job that lets me work from home, pays a good salary, and keeps my identity confidential? What more do you want?"

Mitch waves his arm at Jean, signaling her to move away from the TV.

"I want you to have a respected position that we all can be proud of."

"Listen, I've held a respected role as a wife, mother, budget analyst, seamstress, negotiator, cook, server, and anything else that requires oversight in this house! Now, I'm asking you politely to back off, and if you truly want to help me, pray!"

Mitch watches Jean as she storms off. Feeling frustrated, he leans back on the couch and begins flipping through different TV channels. Soon, he sees reports of the impending fiscal crisis across several news networks. Annoyed, he wonders why his voice carries significant influence nationwide yet seems not to affect his wife.

At Paul's apartment, the same news report echoes from the TV. Paul shouts to his wife in the kitchen as he walks to the living room.

"Kelly, did you hear what was just said on TV? It reflects everything I warned my audience about over the past three years. You can't lower income taxes for everyone in the country while simultaneously increasing spending and expect there to be no consequences. Now, we might be heading for a crisis, with people cutting back on their spending and businesses considering layoffs."

As Paul sits down in the living room, he shouts for his sons. "Preston and Pierce, come in here!"

The sounds of doors opening and closing resonate throughout the hallways as both Preston and Pierce approach their father.

"What's going on, Dad?"

"Boys, we might be heading toward a financial crisis in this country. I mentioned it on my show earlier today. Did you get a chance to listen?"

Both Preston and Pierce shake their heads no.

Paul rubs his head in frustration.

"Well, maybe if you guys weren't always practicing for that great career as professional gamers, you'd know that the economic market, even for pro gamers, is about to change. That is why I am looking forward to you meeting my good friend, Mr. Sinclair. He just emailed me to say there are two openings for summer internships."

Pierce can't believe what he is hearing.

"Really, Dad? I thought we told you we did not want to go to some government program."

Paul looks at his sons.

"I don't care what you said! We've already discussed this."

Preston and Pierce mumble to themselves as they leave the room. Paul glances at them, shakes his head, and shouts toward the kitchen.

"Kelly, are you sure these are my kids?" He's joking. "You know, you were pretty wild in your younger days!"

Kelly sticks her head out of the kitchen and yells back, "Yes, that's true, and that was the last time anything wild happened in my life!"

That's the last Kelly hears from Paul for the rest of the night.

After finishing his drive-time podcast, Tony gets home from his show, drops his bags, and turns on the TV to catch up on the latest updates about the upcoming fiscal crisis. As he walks to the bathroom, he hears snippets of the special report from the National News Center.

Tony paces back and forth and decides to call Nicole.

"Nicole, sweetheart, how are you doing?"

The clang of pots and pans can be heard in the background as Nicole washes dishes.

"Hey, Tony, I'm doing great. How was your day?"

Tony walks into his kitchen and over to the refrigerator, looking for something to eat.

"Hectic! As you probably already know, all hell is breaking loose in the financial industry."

Nicole says, "Yes, I've been seeing special reports flash on my TV. I rely on you to sift through the nonsense and give me the truth. How bad is it?"

Tony pulls out some leftovers from the refrigerator and places them on the counter.

"The situation could become quite serious. It all depends on how the financial sector reacts to the economic changes. If they think the downturn will be brief, we might see a quick recovery. However, if they believe the fiscal chaos will persist indefinitely, they might start pulling funds from various parts of the economy, making recovery difficult."

Nicole nervously fumbles a pot against the sink as she attentively listens.

"No matter how you see it, sweetheart, everyone will feel the pain if this keeps going on too long." Speaking of pain, how's Jason doing? He texted me to say he was finally called for an interview with the young man he met at the bar. Did he go to the interview?"

Nicole finishes the dishes and sits at the kitchen table.

"Yes, he did, Tony."

Tony smiles. "Well, how did it go?"

Nicole hesitates, then answers.

"According to Jason, he did well. He told the interviewer that he was looking for a company that values its employees and provides a positive experience for its customers."

Tony places some food on a plate and heads to the microwave. "So, what happened?"

Nicole smiles. "He must have done well because they called Jason three days later and offered him a job."

Tony places his food in the microwave and smiles. "They offered him a job!"

Nicole, still smiling, says, "Yes, Tony, he was offered the job."

Tony claps as he shuts the microwave door.

"Yes! Nicole, you know what that means!"

Nicole listens carefully. "No, what does that mean?"

"It means that you and I will finally be alone when Jason gets his own place!"

The room falls silent as Nicole remains quiet.

"Nicole, are you there?"

Nicole finally responds. "Yes, Tony, I'm here."

"What happened?"

Nicole speaks slowly. "Jason turned down the job."

"Jason did what?"

"Jason turned down the job!"

Tony forgets about his food in the microwave and sits down at his kitchen table.

"Nicole, what the hell is going on? Why would he do that?"

Nicole stands up, rearranges the flowers in the center of the table, and begins pacing the floor.

"Listen, Tony, don't start! He made his decision, and I'm okay with it."

Tony jumps up and starts pacing the floor.

"Are you truly okay with that decision? Did he mention that he met the business owner and that they got along very well? Did he say that the owner has a contract with President Hale to manage his social media campaign?"

Nicole stands there holding her phone. "No, Tony, he didn't tell me that."

Tony sits back down at the table.

"So, what was his excuse for turning down the job of a lifetime?"

Nicole hesitates and then softly says, "He mentioned that while the company's values aligned with his regarding social and environmental responsibility, they offered him a starting salary of only $63,000 a year. He felt this was too low for the energy, time, and skills he would bring to the role. Also, he expressed concern that the company might require him to work some weekends, which he believed would hurt his work-life balance, something he considers essential for his happiness."

Tony's mouth gapes open. "Nicole, the young man hasn't worked since he graduated from college. I can't help but wonder what skills he has to offer, aside from his daily routine of eating and sleeping."

Nicole says nothing.

"So, what did you say when he told you that nonsense?"

Nicole, feeling somewhat embarrassed, softly says, "I told him I want him to be happy."

"That's it? That's all you told him?"

"Yes."

Tony wishes he could talk to Nicole in person.

"Why didn't you call me when it first happened? I could have talked to him."

Nicole continues to pace the floor, circling her kitchen table.

"I was worried you might have been too harsh on him, especially since he had just turned down the position. He was feeling sensitive about the entire situation, and I didn't want him to feel any worse."

Tony walks into his living room and sits on the couch.

"Are you really concerned about the feelings of a nearly thirty-year-old man who has graduated from college, doesn't work, doesn't pay any bills, and still lives with his mother? Let me ask you this: Who will take care of you when you need support?"

The silence between the two phones is deafening until Nicole gathers the courage to say, "Tony, everything you say might be true, but you have to understand where I'm coming from. He is my only son, and he is here for me."

Tony is confused.

"What are you talking about? I'm here for you!"

Nicole wipes tears from her eyes.

"No! Jason is here for me! You're here at your convenience!"

Tony is stunned and almost drops the phone.

"Where did all of this come from?"

Nicole gets a tissue from the other side of the room.

"Ten years of waiting for you to commit."

Tony does not say a word.

"Jason may be slacking in some areas, but he's here, and he's consistent. That is something I cannot say about you."

Then, in a bold move, the phone goes dead.

14

Acceptance

Early Monday morning in July, Paul drives his sons to the Eastern Sector National Research Center in upstate New York to start their internships. As they get closer to their destination, Paul warns them:

"Boys, you have a great chance to learn from Mr. Sinclair. I have known him for many years, even when he was working as a government intern. Now, he is the senior research engineer responsible for AI development and its effects on efficiency and security."

Paul arrives forty-five minutes later and drives up to the guard's gate.

"Good morning, my name is Paul Vorbont, and we're here to see Mr. Sinclair."

The guard looks at Paul, then runs his fingers through some pages.

"Yes, sir, Mr. Vorbont, I see your name here with two others. Please put this visitor pass in your window, and park in the visitor lot on your right."

As Paul pulls into the parking lot, he turns to his sons.

"Listen, guys, I won't be going in with you. You're young men, and I expect you to act like adults. Please show Mr. Sinclair the respect he deserves, and make sure that I don't receive any negative reports upon my return. Do you understand?"

Preston, frustrated, looks at his father. "Yes, sir. Whatever you say, Dad."

The boys walk into the building and down a long corridor. The lobby is massive, with unadorned walls and dim lighting. There are no chairs for people to sit, as the security ropes guide Preston and Pierce to the security desk.

"We are Preston and Pierce Vorbont, and we're here to see Mr. Sinclair."

The guard checks his paperwork, confirms their names, and hands out visitors' passes to attach to their shirts.

"Gentlemen, keep these tags on as long as you're in this building, and when your internship ends, you must return them to this desk. Do you understand?"

Preston and Pierce respond in unison, "Yes, sir."

The guard gives them directions as they put on their tags.

"All right, guys, go down that hallway and turn right at the corner. You'll find a door labeled 'Exploration Division.' Mr. Sinclair is waiting for you there."

Preston nervously smiles at the guard. "Thank you."

Preston and Pierce follow the guard's instructions and approach the door labeled "Exploration Division." Upon entering, they are greeted by a room filled with enormous computers and database servers. The room is noisy, and the sound of the HVAC units cooling the room hums in the background. About twenty-five people work in the central area, while ten others focus on a project at the back of the room. Preston and Pierce stand at the entrance, gazing around in amazement.

When Mr. Sinclair notices them at the door, he walks over.

"You guys are Paul's boys?"

"Yes, sir."

"Listen, your father is a good man. He stood up for me back in 2000, when predictions were that all the computers you see here would crash because of the Y2K bug. A significant amount of money and overtime were spent to prevent a nationwide computer failure. However, when the crash didn't occur, the government wanted to fire everyone in our department. It was your father, on his radio program, who defended us. He made such a strong case for government workers that officials reconsidered their plans, and here I am today! I personally called his show to thank him, and we have been good friends ever since."

Pierce and Paul appear impressed.

"All right, guys, let me show you around."

Mr. Sinclair begins walking through his expansive department, pointing to various sections where he works on AI projects for different government sectors.

"Gentlemen, I won't show you every part of AI development because some of it is boring, and I know you guys have no patience for dullness."

Mr. Sinclair smiles as he takes Preston and Pierce to another sector that has red glass doors.

"This restricted area is designated for special projects, usually commissioned by the president or his senior advisers. In fact, I currently have three researchers running analysis reports for a specific request. I would let you see what's happening, but that would mean I'd have to have you terminated."

Stunned, Preston and Pierce exchanged wide-eyed glances, looking at each other in disbelief.

Mr. Sinclair sees their reaction and laughs.

"Come on, guys, I was just joking! But honestly, even if someone leaves that red door open, you're not allowed to go in. Do you understand?"

"Yes, sir."

Mr. Sinclair heads to another area of the building.

"Great, now, follow me. Since you're Paul's guys, you will work in three critical sections focused on integrating AI into their projects. Follow me to the cybersecurity section."

Mr. Sinclair, Preston, and Pierce walk down a corridor until they reach two massive doors. Mr. Sinclair steps in front of them and presses a red button. The double doors swing open, revealing a small city of people working at computer terminals surrounding a huge monitor screen set in the middle of the floor, displaying the nations of the world. Stunned by the sight, Pierce and Preston exchange looks.

Pierce gently taps Preston on the shoulder. "Do you know how good our gaming skills could be if we had one of those screens in our basement?"

Preston smiles. "Yeah, we could rock the gaming industry!"

Mr. Sinclair overhears them and says, "Come on, guys, are you serious? Look around the room. These scientists and engineers are among the best in the nation, and their primary role is to protect the eastern corridor from cyber threats. There's no professional gaming without the protection these individuals provide."

Mr. Sinclair turns and walks toward another door.

"Follow me. I have another area that may be of interest."

Mr. Sinclair leads Preston and Paul to a heavy glass door. He presses a red button on the wall, and the door opens. As Preston and Pierce look around, another giant monitor in the middle of the room captivates them.

Mr. Sinclair pauses to observe the activity in the room before turning to Preston.

"All right, gentlemen, this is an area of great interest to your father. It's a room where scientists evaluate and study the effects of climate change. They use artificial intelligence to assess the long-term impacts of this phenomenon and determine how much of it is caused by human activities versus natural occurrences."

Mr. Sinclair continues speaking as he walks past the monitor and the computer terminals spread throughout the floor.

"The use of AI is crucial because politicians from both sides are seeking more reliable ways to analyze the data we collect and understand its impact. We have several satellites monitoring the Earth's ozone layer, which protects humanity by identifying vulnerabilities in its ability to shield our planet from ultraviolet radiation."

Preston and Pierce look bored.

"Now, let's move on to the final part of your internship, which I promise will interest you."

He leads them down a long corridor, then steps outside. They continue a few more feet to a building on a hill that resembles an airplane hangar.

"Are you guys ready?"

Preston and Pierce, thinking this is another boring presentation, say, "Yes, we're ready."

Mr. Sinclair swipes his ID badge on the wall terminal, and the double doors slide open, revealing the largest radar antenna ever built. Preston and Pierce's eyes widen. Then Mr. Sinclair presses a red button on the wall, and the roof of the building opens. The sun shines brightly down onto the radar antenna as Pierce and Preston marvel at the sky.

"Come on, guys, I know the beauty of the Earth and its features is irresistible, but I have one more thing to show you."

They walk through a second set of double doors into a dimly lit room. Mr. Sinclair approaches the wall and presses a green button. As the roof retracts again, he turns on the lights, revealing the largest telescope they have ever seen.

Preston looks at Pierce, and Pierce looks back at Preston. He can say only one thing: "Wow!"

Mr. Sinclair walks over to Preston and Pierce.

"This, gentlemen, is the largest and most significant space telescope ever built. It can observe into space millions of light-years away and record various celestial objects and anomalies that may be of interest to our nation. The amazing thing is that it doesn't require someone to be present to monitor space."

Preston and Pierce walk around the telescope's base, amazed by its size. Mr. Sinclair smiles as he sees that he has gotten their attention.

"Guys, do you know what's really amazing? We're currently integrating the next level of AI technology into our systems. It's called *Cohesive Adaptive Space Technology Intelligence*."

Preston attentively listens to Mr. Sinclair as he continues his tour of the facility.

"We know about AI, but what is *Cohesive Adaptive Space Technology Intelligence?*"

Mr. Sinclair stops and turns his attention to Preston.

"Cohesive Adaptive Space Technology Intelligence, or CAST-I, involves integrating AI platforms from around the world and cross-referencing their data to generate multiple references from diverse sources. The strength of CAST-I lies in its ability to combine these sources into a single, primary source, producing an outcome that is more comprehensive and powerful than any individual AI platform available today. CAST-I provides our government with combined data that will enhance our technology platform, access previously unavailable information, and improve our ability to defend our nation's interests."

Preston and Pierce stand frozen with intrigue.

"So, what does that mean for space exploration? Well, in a few months, we'll incorporate CAST-I into our space exploration program. It'll produce the most potent signal ever sent into space, and the best part is that it'll connect and synchronize the most sensitive telescope on Earth with the most sensitive telescopes in space. The result will provide us with the deepest view of space ever recorded."

Pierce stares at Mr. Sinclair, feeling confused and somewhat worried.

"What if something is out there? Do we really want them to know we're here?"

Preston, realizing that his brother has a good point, says, "That's right, and even if we contact someone, are we ready to deal with them? What if they're trying to attack us with weapons we've never heard of?"

Mr. Sinclair looks at Preston and Pierce, impressed.

"You guys aren't as laid-back as I thought you were."

Mr. Sinclair, aware that the young men's questions spark serious debates among the military's top ranks, shifts the subject.

"Listen, it's time for lunch. Let's take a break, and then I'll show you with whom and where you'll be working when your internship begins."

In the fourth year of Hale's presidency, the economy experiences a significant downturn, causing shockwaves throughout the nation. Families everywhere see the troubling financial news broadcast on their TVs, and President Hale believes it is the right time to address the nation.

"Dear family and friends, when I first ran for office, I made five major commitments aimed at improving your lives. Despite facing significant opposition from Congress, I successfully carried out every part of my plan. Tax reduction, education, health care, defense spending, and family values are the core of my beliefs and my identity."

In an unprecedented move, the president rises from his chair, walks to the front of his desk, and looks into the camera as if he is engaging in a friendly conversation with the nation.

"My five-point policy plan was so successful that it sparked a nationwide increase in spending, which was well deserved. Yes, the high demand for products and services led to price hikes. However, it was the business community's response to that increased demand that surprised my administration. Instead of expanding their businesses and hiring more employees to accommodate the demand, they chose to maintain their current workforce and enjoy higher profit margins. That decision resulted in inflation affecting the entire nation.

As the president walks around his office, the camera follows him as he continues to speak.

"I'll never regret putting more money in your pockets because it's your money, not mine or Congress's. Since I became president, the average American has seen their income tax rates drop by thirty percent across the board. It's an unprecedented tax reduction not seen since 1981. My only regret is that I assumed the business community would support my agenda, especially after I lowered corporate taxes. Although we may experience a period of economic adjustment, I am confident that we will emerge from this challenging time stronger than ever.

The president walks toward his desk and takes his seat, with the camera following him.

"My administration takes full responsibility for the current state of our economy. I hope you will give us time to address this issue and restore our economy to its position as the greatest in the world. Have a good night."

15
Breakdown

Six months after the president's address, the economy continues to decline. Financial markets respond negatively to a significant drop in consumer spending. Businesses are feeling the pressure of the economic crisis, leading advertisers to cut their budgets.

Mitch is preparing to begin his show as Jake hurries into his studio.

"Mitch, I have some bad news to share. Three of your top ten sponsors have canceled their sponsorship due to low sales. They apologized and asked to be considered for future advertising slots when sales pick up."

Mitch makes eye contact with Jake and shrugs his shoulders.

"No problem. Most of my top supporters have been with me for years, so I can't be too upset with them. We'll find a way to accommodate them when things improve. However, without their financial support, are we still able to operate within our budget?"

"Yes, sir."

Mitch waves his hand and shoos Jake out of the booth. Jake strolls into the control room, looks through the glass, and picks up his microphone.

"All right, let's start the show!"

Mitch sits upright in his chair as the lights dim in the studio, and Jake starts the countdown: "Five, four, three, two, one."

Mitch leans into the microphone and starts speaking live from his studio:

"Welcome! You're listening to the one and only *Consultant of Conservatism* on WCONS in New York City. I'm the top conservative talk show host in the country, with over three hundred stations carrying my show."

Mitch leans back and begins his monologue.

"Ladies and gentlemen, let's get straight to the point. We're currently facing a fiscal crisis, which I predicted would happen when President Hale was elected. Unfortunately, no one has listened to my advice, and now we're seeing the effects of his naivete on a national scale. Sales are falling, prices are climbing, and unemployment is rising. This is the perfect storm of a crisis that will inevitably lead to a recession. My producer told me just before this show that three of my sponsors had to pull out due to a weakening retail market and low sales."

Mitch pauses angrily and stares at Jake.

"Family, this is what happens when you deal with a president who promotes a five-point plan that lacks substance. You've been misled by a people-pleaser who does not understand the importance of his policies or what happens when one policy affects another. Our nation is now facing a potential recession, and if that happens, chaos will spread across the city."

Mitch's face reflected his frustration as he slammed his hand on the desk.

"Did you hear what the president said in his address to the nation? He took responsibility for his failed policies but urged the country to reelect him so that he could address the issues he had created. That, ladies and gentlemen, sounds like crazy talk from a crazy president! Why would anyone elect a president who is leading the country into a recession? I don't understand it!"

As Mitch continued, Jake notified him that they need to take a break.

"Listen, family, we need to take a break, but stay tuned. We'll be back after hearing from the few sponsors who have stayed loyal to this show!"

Making sure they're on a break, Jake grabs a microphone and talks to Mitch through the speaker.

"Mitch, was that last comment necessary? We need all our sponsors to feel confident that there will be no repercussions if they drop out due to financial difficulties. We can't afford to lose any more sponsors!"

Mitch gazes at Jake with curiosity.

"How many sponsors in total dropped out?"

Jake sifts through the papers on his desk.

"Five."

Mitch stares at Jake in frustration as Jake brings the show back from the break. Annoyed, Mitch leans into the microphone.

"Family, I want to update you that as of today, five of my sponsors have withdrawn their support because of the president and his misguided five-point plan. Although the purpose of this show is to provide information and entertainment, it must also be profitable. No matter how much you enjoy listening to me, if we don't generate revenue for the corporate side, we risk facing serious consequences. The bottom line is, without sponsors, there's no show."

Angry, Mitch stands up from his desk and looks at Jake.

"We're going to take an early break. That's right, Jake; I'm taking my own breaks. We'll be right back after a word from the only loyal sponsors we have left!"

Stunned, Jake jumps up from his chair and hurries to find a sponsor for the break. He loads the commercial and keys his microphone.

"Come on, Mitch, go easy on the sponsors; I really need this job!"

In the meantime, Paul argues with Rochelle after discovering that three of his top seven sponsors have ended their partnerships. She assures him that the decision is not personal and has nothing to do with the show's content; it is purely financial.

Paul anxiously prepares to start his show, feeling frustrated and worried about its future. As his intro music begins, his thoughts drift, knowing that his show's funding is in jeopardy.

"America! Welcome to WPROG in New York City, the top nationally syndicated liberal talk show host in the country. I'm an open-minded, freethinking, generous citizen who loves our country and supports the rights of all Americans, regardless of race, creed, color, or gender."

Paul leans forward in his chair.

"Listen, everyone, I won't sugarcoat what's happening in our nation. We're in serious trouble! Just a few years ago, people were thriving, feeling good, and spending freely. Now, we're facing a major recession that could cripple the economy."

Paul's frustration is evident on his face as he continues.

"For the past twenty years, I have been open with you, and I won't hide my feelings now. I'm uncertain about the future of this program, particularly given the number of sponsors dropping out. Let me be clear: This situation isn't a reflection of our programming's quality; it's due to the economic crisis affecting both the public and the business community."

Paul takes a sip of water.

"In a strong economy, if one program shuts down, another station usually picks it up because many sponsors are eager to advertise. However, during a recession, few sponsors are willing to invest in advertising for a program until they see signs of economic recovery. As a result, live programming is paused, and reruns or 'best of' programs air until funding resumes. In other words, if this recession lasts for any significant period, I could lose my job. That, my friends, is the truth, honest and transparent."

Rochelle puts up the sign for a break.

"Ladies and gentlemen, we'll be right back after a word from the few loyal sponsors left who have the guts to support this program."

Rochelle goes to break, grabs a microphone, and speaks to Paul.

"Paul, let's cut the sponsors some slack."

Paul glares at Rochelle through the glass.

"Cut them some slack? We generated millions for those sponsors, and now that the economists have predicted a recession, they're pulling out. Yes, things look bad, but a recession has not been officially declared!"

Paul stands up, grabs the microphone, and glares at Rochelle through the glass.

"I'm fed up with being loyal to everyone while no one shows loyalty to us. Those sponsors came into our offices and practically begged us to let them advertise on our station. We welcomed them with open arms. When they couldn't afford the advertising fees, we divided their time slots into more affordable segments and even let them air on weekend nights. But when an economic stall is predicted, the first thing they cut is our show's advertising. They are some ungrateful bastards!"

Rochelle, reminiscing about those times, nods in agreement, then turns to the control board. "You're right."

She raises her hand in the air to start the show.

"Here we go! Five, four, three, two, one."

As Tony prepares for his show, he scans the latest news updates and hears Mitch and Paul vent about their sponsors. Feeling a bit anxious, he glances at Rob.

"How are we doing in reference to our sponsors?"

Rob smiles as he looks at Tony from across the studio.

"Right now, we're doing well. We don't have much overhead, so we can lose a few sponsors and still produce a quality program."

Tony has a relieved look on his face as he smiles.

"That's great. How long can we last, even with the low overhead?"

Rob shakes his head and chuckles at Tony's worries.

"Listen, Tony, you have the top podcast in the country. Even if you only have three sponsors left, we can run the program from your living room if needed and still succeed."

Tony smiles.

"I appreciate you, but it appears there's an economic crisis headed our way, and I want to be prepared if things get worse and no money is coming in."

Rob shakes his head, seeing that Tony is overthinking the situation.

"Come on, Tony, we've been through difficulties before and always managed to get through them. I understand that the internet is different from traditional radio. Still, the worst-case scenario I can picture is a total failure of the internet infrastructure, which would leave most of us without any way to communicate."

Tony has a worried expression on his face.

"Well, what if that happens? Do we have a backup plan?"

Rob's expression changes as he contemplates the question.

"It's not just your program that would encounter serious issues. If the internet were to collapse, it could lead to chaos worldwide. As for backups, there are no real alternatives for us unless we're fortunate enough to have access to satellite communications."

Tony looks concerned, gripped by Rob's premise.

"Now you've got me confused! How is it that we have no backup for primary internet services?"

Rob says, "Although backups do exist, most remain connected to the digital highway. A true backup system must be built independently of the internet, and that would cost us a lot of money."

Not satisfied, Tony says, "All right, that's enough of that discussion. Let's get back to planning the show, since I have plenty to cover."

16
Bittersweet Home

Mitch drives home to Long Island, stops for gas, and is shocked by the sudden price hike.

"How is it that premium gas was \$3.40 per gallon two days ago and has now jumped to \$4.99 per gallon? This doesn't make sense! It's the same gas that was in the tanks two days ago!"

Unfortunately, Mitch has no choice but to pay because it's the last station before getting on the Long Island Expressway. While he is filling up his tank, his wife calls.

"I know you must be happy!"

"Jean, what are you talking about?"

Jean is crying. "I just got a call from my manager informing me that all foot models will be laid off because of low sales."

Mitch has a slight grin on his face as Jean continues.

"Even more troubling, I've heard from my colleagues that the company does not intend to rehire us once the economy recovers. Instead, they plan to replace us with AI-generated models that can be tailored to meet customer needs."

Mitch's grin grows wider. He finishes pumping gas and sarcastically says, "How can they do that? You know, they really don't appreciate your services."

"Oh, shut up, Mitch! I know you must be jumping for joy, but remember, it's my job first. AI will replace talk radio programs later."

Mitch places the gas pump back into its holder.

"Sweetheart, that's not going to happen. My name is Mitch Corvane, and you're married to the top radio host in the country. It'll take more than AI to match my skills!"

Jean listens in frustration.

"Thanks for your arrogance and empathy!"

As Mitch gets into his car, he closes the door.

"Wait a minute, Jean, you misunderstood—"

Jean hangs up. Mitch shouts into the phone: "Jean? Jean!"

Mitch bangs on the steering wheel in frustration, starts his car, and drives toward the entrance ramp for the Long Island Expressway, dreading what awaits him when he gets home.

It's 6:45 p.m., and Paul is heading home. As he walks into his apartment, Kelly greets him at the door with a kiss.

"It's good to see you, Paul. How was your day?"

Paul looks at Kelly with a discouraging expression.

"Honestly, it was one of the worst broadcasts I've had since I started broadcasting."

Kelly looks confused. "Let me guess. Your program was mostly about the fiscal disaster heading our way."

Paul takes off his jacket.

"All day, that was the topic. It was frustrating, and to top it off, we lost three sponsors!"

Kelly walks Paul over to the living room and sits down next to him.

"Paul, it gets worse. Given the current atmosphere, people are rushing to the bank to withdraw large sums of cash to protect themselves in case the banks shut down. What's remarkable is that the banks don't have enough money to cover their depositors' demands, so they're asking many customers to return the next day."

Jeans shook her head.

"But you know how people are: Some don't trust the banks, so I heard on the radio that people are sleeping on the ground, waiting for the banks to open."

Paul stares at Kelly and shakes his head as she continues.

"To make matters worse, there are rumors that the banks may limit the amount of funds anyone can withdraw, regardless of how much money they have in their accounts."

Paul pauses and shakes his head in disbelief as his mind wanders to another topic.

"Where are the boys?"

"I guess they're in their rooms."

Paul yells from the living room. "Preston and Pierce, come out here!"

The echo of doors opening and closing precedes Preston and Pierce's entrance into the living room.

"Yes, sir."

Paul stands up to address his sons.

"Boys, I appreciate your participation in the government internship over the past year. However, Mr. Sinclair requested that you come to the center next Saturday. Due to the current economic crisis, Mr. Sinclair is likely working on solutions to the financial issues we are experiencing. I need you to pay close attention to any information that could be beneficial for us."

Kelly is startled as she stares at Paul.

"Paul, what are you asking? Do you want them to snoop around a government facility?"

Paul glances at Kelly and acts like he's offended by her question.

"What? Of course not! However, if they overhear anything that would be helpful, I'd appreciate it."

Preston looks confused, but Pierce speaks up, thinking he understands his father's request. "Oh, you mean like the red room that helps the president make decisions?"

Paul's eyes widen. "Really? Is there such a room?"

Preston, aware that Pierce has said too much, says, "Pierce, that's enough! Dad, we'll let you know if we hear anything."

Paul gives Preston an annoyed look, thinking Pierce was going to provide him with some inside information.

"All right, boys, forget what I said. You can go back to your rooms."

Kelly is surprised and confused when Paul dismisses the boys.

"You made a big deal about the family eating together. Why didn't you make them stay for dinner?"

Paul smiles.

"I didn't want to upset them. I want them to keep their eyes and ears open around Mr. Sinclair."

Kelly stares at Paul in disbelief.

"It sounds like you're using them as your personal spies."

Paul snaps back, "Heck, they have been using me for the past eighteen years. They owe me!"

It's 9:30 p.m., and Tony is finishing his show. As he packs his bags, he receives a call from Nicole.

"I know tonight is the night when you come over and eat dinner, but I'm not in the mood for company."

Tony hears the concern in her voice. "Nicole, what's wrong?"

Nicole pauses to gather her thoughts.

"I just lost my job as a senior finance analyst."

Tony is stunned. Nicole has worked in that position for over twenty years.

"No … what happened?"

Tears run down Nicole's face as she tries to explain.

"Our manager gathered everyone in the meeting room to clarify that the layoffs are not due to performance issues. Instead, they're a necessary response to the current economic situation, which requires budget cuts. I also heard in the lunchroom that the company plans to use AI to improve cost control and enhance data reporting."

Tony listens and says nothing as Nicole continues.

"Tony, I feel lost. I've spent years dedicated to this company, and with the current economy, who would hire a fiscal analyst now?"

Tony sighs. "You're right; finding a job in your field is tough right now. I urge you not to make any decisions until things settle down. Have you talked to Jason?"

Nicole sits down as she continues.

"Yes, I did, and he was distraught, so much that he stormed out of the house and said he was going to Times Square to join the protest over the economy."

Tony is stunned.

"You mean to tell me that he is going out to protest job layoffs when he has never held a job?"

Nicole dislikes Tony's tone and feels the need to defend her son's actions.

"Well, at least he is trying to do something to support his mother."

Tony laughs. "Really? Wouldn't a job be the best thing he could do to support his mother?"

Nicole does not like the direction the conversation is going.

"I wanted some understanding and sympathy for my situation. Instead, you decide to criticize me for my son's actions, which he believes are justified. There are thousands of people in Times Square standing up for those harmed by this economy."

Tony realizes he's gotten distracted and thrown off by Jason's actions.

"I'm sorry, Nicole. You're right. We'll get through this situation together, and I truly mean together. This economic downturn won't last long, and in the meantime, I'll do everything I can to support you."

Nicole wipes the tears from her face.

"Thank you, Tony. I appreciate you."

Tony gets up from his chair and heads for his vehicle.

"No problem, sweetheart. Get some rest, and we'll talk tomorrow. Good night!"

17

Outrage

Three months before the election, candidates from both the Republican and Democratic parties are in full campaign mode as the economy faces a severe downturn. Each candidate believes that the struggling economy will work in their favor, especially with protests erupting across the country.

Meanwhile, President Hale is noticeably absent from campaigning as his adviser walks into his office.

"Mr. President, the public and the media are questioning whether you have lost hope since your last address to the nation. People are sleeping on the sidewalks outside banks, waiting to access their money, and some are rushing to supermarkets to hoard essential goods. News reports show that the supermarket shelves are bare and empty, and panic is spreading among the population."

President Hale looks up at Mr. Bishop.

"Don't you think I know what's going on? I saw the news and the protests in Times Square. Unfortunately, there's nothing I can do. Congress isn't interested in acting because they're focused on their election campaigns, and they want me out. Let's be honest, Mr. Bishop: There's no way I can win reelection under these circumstances."

The president stands up from his desk.

"Everything is falling apart much sooner than anticipated, and immediate action is needed to preserve what remains of our mission. We tried to operate subtly to integrate into the system while still focusing on our agenda. However, this political structure is so unpredictable that it's challenging to implement anything without encountering objections from outside interests."

The president walks to Mr. Bishop.

"You know, Mr. Bishop, there's a saying here: Desperate times call for desperate measures. Contact Mr. Sinclair and gauge his mindset by suggesting possible changes to his research projects, particularly his space program. See if he is willing to cooperate. If not, do what you must to halt the process."

Mr. Bishop nods in agreement, then changes the subject.

"Mr. President, I hate to bring this up, but I have some more bad news for you."

President Hale rolls his eyes as he walks back to his desk and sits down.

"The International Nations of Finance gathered earlier today to discuss our nation's fiscal health and how it affects their economies. They expressed serious concern about the financial losses during this downturn and are contemplating withdrawing significant resources from our Treasury."

President Hale stares at Mr. Bishop in disbelief, taking in the weight of what he is hearing.

"Did you explain to them that this nation has gone through several recessions but has always come out stronger? Did you emphasize that there's no better place for their investment than in this great nation? Did you mention that the current situation results from a system of checks and balances that will eventually make the necessary corrections to position us at the forefront of the global economy? Did you tell them that if they decide to withdraw their funding from this nation, we'll remember their actions when we recover, and that won't be favorable for them?"

Mr. Bishop listens attentively to the president as he speaks and responds thoughtfully.

"No, sir, I did not tell them that exactly. But I did say there would be consequences for their actions."

Mr. Bishop's phone rings in the middle of their conversation, and the president's adviser listens for more than two minutes. Puzzled, the President wonders what is happening.

"Mr. President, twenty key nations are looking to withdraw their money from our Treasury."

The president rises from his desk and stares intently at Mr. Bishop.

"Really! So, these twenty nations are willing to ignore the strength and resiliency of this nation's economy and withdraw their money, anyway?"

"I guess so, Mr. President."

President Hale looks at Mr. Bishop.

"Gather our economic advisers and have them meet me in the Position Room in four hours. This includes Mr. Sinclair, who should have that fiscal analysis ready for me."

Mr. Bishop hurries and packs his bag.

"Yes, sir, Mr. President."

Four hours later, the Position Room is filled with advisers and experts. However, three hours into the meeting, the president expresses frustration with the recommended suggestions.

"This meeting is over! I'm in the final stages of my candidacy, and everyone here is discussing long-term solutions. I need short-term results, which no one here can provide. So, I will decide on my own!"

The president stands up and walks around the table as everyone, including Mr. Sinclair, waits to hear his proposal.

"I'll instruct the head of the Treasury to freeze all foreign accounts until further notice. If any of the twenty or more key nations divests its funds, it could trigger an economic crisis from which we may never recover. By freezing all foreign accounts, we can stabilize the economy while we work to resolve this economic crisis."

Surprised by the President's suggestion, no one dares to comment on his recommendation except Mr. Bishop.

"Mr. President, if we follow your request to withhold funds from major nations, could that be considered a hostile act? What would be the repercussions of such an action?"

The president squints his eyes and stares at Mr. Bishop in anger.

"I don't give a damn what they think! We're the strongest nation on the planet, and we're asking for their patience as we navigate through this economic crisis! If they're unwilling to cooperate, then that's their choice."

The room is silent as the President paces back and forth across the Presidential Seal.

"Does anyone else have anything else to say?"

The president looks around the room and waits.

"Great, have a good day. Mr. Bishop, meet me in my office."

Mr. Bishop shakes his head as he packs his bag, dreading his upcoming conversation with the president.

It's Saturday night, and Mitch is at home, watching TV in his living room, when a special report interrupts his show.

"Good evening. This is a special report from the National News Center in New York. We have received information that, in addition to the ongoing economic crisis affecting the nation, the international community is outraged because President Hale has frozen all their accounts, limiting access to their funds. Words like *retaliation* and *retribution* are being used as countries to decide on a response to President Hale's actions.

In an unprecedented escalation, the president's adviser, Caldrin Bishop, notes that the nation cannot allow foreign interests to withdraw funds that could push this country into an even deeper fiscal crisis."

Mitch is stunned that the five-point plan has now escalated into an international crisis. He shouts for Jean.

"Jean! Please come and listen to this."

Jean rushes into the living room as the special report repeats.

Mitch looks at her in frustration.

"This is insane! We began three years ago with a spending spree led by the president and now face the possibility of war."

"Don't quote me, but it reminds me of that Scripture that says something like, 'You will hear of wars and rumors of wars . . . Nation will rise against nation, and kingdom against kingdom.'"

Mitch picks up the remote, turns off the television, and stares at Jean.

I don't know what's happening, but I feel uneasy about this.

18

The Call

I t's Saturday, and Paul is taking his boys to the Eastern Sector National Research Center at Mr. Sinclair's request. As they pull up to the guard's gate and into the parking lot, Paul smiles at his sons.

"All right, boys, enjoy your day, and stay alert in case any important information comes your way that you'd want to share with your father."

Preston and Pierce exchange glances and roll their eyes as they step out of the car. Preston then turns and looks at his father.

"Thanks, Dad. We'll see you later."

As Preston and Pierce enter the government facility, they sign in at the guard desk and proceed down the hall to the research division. Upon their arrival, Mr. Sinclair greets them warmly with a friendly smile and guides them along a long, dimly lit corridor. After a short walk, he opens the door to the large airport hangar housing the space exploration program.

Mr. Sinclair swipes his ID badge at the wall terminal, and the double doors slide open. He then turns on the lights.

"Preston and Pierce, welcome back. I'm glad to see you again. However, I have some bad news. We just received word that the nationwide internship program has been canceled due to a lack of funding."

Preston and Pierce exchange glances, uncertain of how to feel.

"I wanted to tell you guys in person instead of sending a letter to your house because of what your father did for me. I also wanted to show you the results of the time you spent here learning AI technology. So, I decided to get a waiver and let you enter this facility one last time."

Preston and Pierce smile at each other as they follow Mr. Sinclair.

"While you're here, I believe it's a great opportunity to provide you with an in-depth look at our space program and how we're implementing Cohesive Adaptive Space Technology Intelligence within our systems. I've accelerated the timeline for this important upgrade due to the current financial situation. What you will witness is innovative, groundbreaking, and unlike anything we have done before."

Preston and Pierce listen with fascination. As they walk through the space facility, Mr. Sinclair shares a theory he has about space.

"All right, guys, your dad cares deeply about fighting global warming and is committed to reducing its effects. I have my own theory about why we need to protect the ozone layer. As you may know, the ozone layer shields us from the sun's harmful UV rays. However, I also believe it might serve as a protective barrier against other intelligent life-forms."

Preston and Pierce raise their eyebrows and look at each other.

"We know that when satellites observe the ozone layer, it appears as a hazy circle surrounding the Earth. It's like an invisible protective ring meant to shield us. I believe one reason a terrestrial entity hasn't approached us is that they can see what we cannot. In other words, I think they might perceive the ozone layer as a force protecting the Earth."

Preston and Pierce stare at Mr. Sinclair in amazement as he finishes his thoughts.

"Listen, guys. I have noticed weakened areas in the ozone layer, and I believe these gaps could make us vulnerable to external threats. About five years ago, a significant incident occurred in space when an unidentified entity disrupted parts of our atmosphere, alarming scientists and researchers. We believe it entered our atmosphere through a spatial gap in the ozone layer, then disappeared instantly. Even now, my researchers are still unable to track and identify that disruption."

Mr. Sinclair has a speculative expression on his face.

"I'm not suggesting that there's a group of aliens planning to attack us. In my view, I don't believe that every unknown entity in the universe is hostile. Some may recognize the value and importance of our planet and try to protect it. Others may have observed breaches in our ozone layer and have entered our atmosphere for reasons we don't yet understand. My concern is that I can address only the openings we currently know about. As the ozone layer continues to deteriorate for reasons that are still unproven, we may be increasing our risk of being approached by external threats."

Pierce looks at Mr. Sinclair. "External threats?"

"Yes, external threats, such as unknown life-forms that may not have our best interests."

Preston and Pierce are intrigued by Mr. Sinclair's theory. They are eager to learn more, but his cell phone rings. Mr. Sinclair recognizes the caller ID and answers. He glances at Preston and Pierce and puts a finger to his lips, signaling them to be quiet. He steps a few feet away from the boys to take the call. However, Mr. Sinclair purposely keeps his phone on speaker so that Preston and Pierce can hear everything being said.

"Good morning, Mr. Bishop. How may I assist you today?"

Mr. Bishop responds, "I know you won't be happy, but we must shut down several research programs until the fiscal crisis ends. One of them is your space exploration program."

Mr. Sinclair is stunned. "But I have invested a significant amount of time in the space research program. I need to activate an AI upgrade to enhance our interactions and view of the universe."

Preston and Pierce watch Mr. Sinclair as he argues with Mr. Bishop over the phone.

"Mr. Sinclair, this shutdown is not an option; it is an order. Now, I expect you to halt the space program until further notice within twenty-four hours."

Mr. Sinclair is shocked. "Twenty-four hours isn't enough time to secure the radar and establish the critical steps needed for remote monitoring! During our last conversation, you asked me to provide an analysis regarding the fiscal crisis. At that time, you mentioned that there was sufficient funding to continue the program. So, what has changed, and why are you making this decision?"

Mr. Bishop reiterates, "Listen closely. Our reasons go far beyond your pay grade and level of understanding. Your desire to contact entities in the universe may not align with those you're trying to reach. You have twenty-four hours, Mr. Sinclair. Do you understand?"

A puzzled and disheartened Mr. Sinclair shifts his gaze between Preston and Pierce as he replies, "Yes, sir."

Mr. Sinclair ends the call, puts his cell phone in his pocket, and heads over to the boys.

"Well, guys, you heard it. I needed someone else to confirm what I was hearing. Not only is the internship program over, but it seems the upgrade to the space program has been put on hold until this fiscal disaster ends."

Mr. Sinclair approaches the giant telescope and looks at it as he considers Mr. Bishop's instructions.

"You know what? To hell with Mr. Bishop's orders! How can he understand the importance of what we're trying to do? You can't turn off science; it's like saying you can turn your brain off. That just isn't possible!"

Then Mr. Sinclair turns and glances at Preston and Pierce.

"Hey, guys! I'm going for it, anyway! By integrating CAST-I into our space program, we'll create the most powerful signal ever sent into space, allowing us to capture the farthest view of the cosmos that the world has ever seen!"

Preston and Pierce exchange a look and then glance at Mr. Sinclair with concern.

"Don't worry, guys. I'm just going to download the CAST-I program, but I won't run it until the funding for the space program is restored."

As Mr. Sinclair turns around to get his laptop, Pierce looks at Preston and whispers, "This is both fascinating and crazy at the same time. I still don't understand why we want to draw attention to ourselves, especially since we don't know what's out there."

Preston whispers, "I agree."

Mr. Sinclair turns and sternly makes eye contact with the boys.

"Listen, what you see me do here stays in here."

Preston and Pierce nod cautiously.

Mr. Sinclair sits at his desk, opens his laptop, and begins installing the CAST-I software. After reviewing his notes, he sets up the CAST-I framework and installs the necessary AI tools to connect the radar software with the telescope's program. Finally, he secures the upgrade by activating the firewalls and adding extra monitoring tools. Then Mr. Sinclair looks at Preston and Pierce and scowls.

"Mr. Bishop is convinced he has all the damn answers, yet he didn't realize I was fully prepared to roll out the AI upgrades in minutes, especially given the fiscal crisis threatening the space program."

Mr. Sinclair disconnects his laptop, walks toward the exit door, and dims the lights.

"Come on, guys, let's get out of here!"

However, before they walk out the door, something bothers Pierce.

"Mr. Sinclair, you mentioned that you would install the software without executing it. Why bother installing it if you're not going to run it?"

"You, my friend, are very perceptive."

As they exit the building, Mr. Sinclair reaches into his pocket, pulls out his smartphone, and opens an app he created.

"I refuse to let government bureaucracy block decades of groundbreaking space exploration, all because of a fiscal crisis caused by our current president."

On his phone, Mr. Sinclair presses the "Deploy and Run" button.

Suddenly, they heard a low-pitched tone emanating from the building, followed by a slow, evenly spaced pulsing sound that gradually increased in speed before merging into a single tone. At that moment, the modified radar sends a burst of CAST-I radio waves into space. As it continues transmitting, the sound fades until it is no longer audible, leaving only a faint hum.

Mr. Sinclair looks at Preston and Pierce and smiles.

"Guys, right now, the most powerful signal ever sent into space is booming across the universe!"

Pierce looks at Preston with excitement.

"Wow! This feels like something you'd see on the Science Fantasy Channel!"

Preston looks at Pierce with concern. "Truthfully, I really don't know what we're seeing or if we should be seeing it."

As they leave the building, Pierce asks Mr. Sinclair, "How long do you think it takes to get any feedback from out there?"

Mr. Sinclair looks at Pierce.

"Honestly, we really don't know. All of this is experimental and unprecedented. But if anything does exist out there, one way or another, we'll find out!"

Pierce looks at Preston.

"Bro, I can't wait until Dad hears this!"

19

The Time Has Come

Two weeks later, the world teeters on the brink of chaos. Former allies are forming a coalition to plan a retaliation strike against the president for freezing their funds. The banking system is on the verge of collapse, and people's debit and credit card accounts have been temporarily frozen. To restore order, the government introduces a three-digit numbering system that will allow individuals to access their bank accounts and government services. Long lines pop up at food distribution centers across the country, leading to looting as people desperately try to provide for their families.

Just when it seems the situation couldn't worsen, Congress learns that President Hale, along with his vice president and senior adviser, has mysteriously vanished. Records show activity in the president's office early in the morning, but by 3:00 p.m., all movements stopped. There is no evidence of foul play or that the president, vice president, or adviser left the building. Their sudden disappearance, which happened without a trace, sends shock waves through a nation already fraught with anxiety and economic uncertainty.

With the growing threat of allied retaliation, Congress warns all countries that any cyberattack or physical attack endangering the nation's core interests will be deemed an act of war and met with a strong response.

As nations around the world gather to protest President Hale's decision to withhold their funds, a powerful force travels through space at an astonishing speed. Its energy is unlike anything humanity has ever encountered, and its presence can be felt throughout the universe as it streaks across the vast expanse of space. Upon entering the Earth's atmosphere, it produces a thunderous boom that stuns world leaders and heads of state as it hovers over the planet as a brilliant light.

While people around the globe pause to watch the light illuminating the sky, anxiety grips the hearts of billions as they fill the streets, overwhelmed by worry and fear.

Amid the illuminated skyline and swirling winds, an audible sound pierces through the clouds. As the light hovers above the Earth's surface, the message is clear to some and inaudible to others. The reason some people hear it while others do not remains a mystery. However, for those who hear it, there is no doubt that the message is real.

Mitch and Jean step onto their deck, stunned by the ominous light hovering over their backyard. To make matters worse, all internet services, as well as TV and phone networks, are down. Unable to comprehend what he is witnessing, Mitch believes the chaos is a sign of the Second Coming.

"Jean, I don't remember the Scriptures as well as I used to, but I recall the Bible mentioning something like: Everyone on Earth will see the Son of Man coming on the clouds of heaven with power and great glory, and He shall judge the living and the dead."

As Jean continues to look up at the light, she says, "I remember hearing something like that in church, but Mitch, what if we are not the only beings out here? What if there are areas of our existence that God never meant for us to understand? What if He didn't reveal everything to us, knowing we would have a hard time understanding it?"

Mitch listens intently to Jean as she continues.

"Basically, I'm asking: What would happen if it turned out we're not alone and what we're looking at is proof of that?"

Just as she finishes speaking, Mitch turns his head as if he's heard something. "Did you hear that?"

Jean looks at Mitch. "No, I didn't hear a thing."

"I heard a voice."

Concerned, Jean stares at Mitch, who glances back, aware that she doesn't believe him. For a few minutes, no one says anything.

As they continue to gaze at the light, thoughts of their daughters come to Mitch's mind. "Jean, I just thought about our daughters!"

Jean looks at Mitch with a helpless expression. "Oh my God! We have no way to check on them to see if they're okay!"

Mitch reaches out to hug Jean, and she pushes him away.

"This is all your damn fault!"

Mitch is stunned. "What? How is this my fault?"

Jean points her finger at Mitch's chest.

"The entire internet infrastructure has collapsed, along with television, phone, and internet services. I warned you that this might happen someday, leaving us unable to communicate with anyone. But you didn't take me seriously. When I asked if I could buy a satellite phone with money from our joint account, you dismissed my concerns as paranoia."

Mitch, looking stunned, says nothing.

"But you know what, Mitch? If I were earning my own money, I would have bought the phone myself and, most likely, would be in contact with my girls right now!"

Frustrated, Jean walks away from Mitch and heads toward the house. Then, she abruptly turns around.

"Listen to me, Mitch Corvane! You need to find a way for me to contact my daughters so I can make sure they're okay. Do you understand!"

Jean, not waiting for Mitch to answer, keeps walking toward the house with tears streaming down her face. Then suddenly, she turns around one last time.

"While you search for my daughters, I'll go inside to pray that the light covering the sky signifies hope and not death!"

Mitch stands alone, reflecting on his life. His celebrated talk show and radio fame now feel empty in light of current events. The rhetoric and political drama he previously shared with his audience seem meaningless as he gazes up at the skyline, and a harsh reality settles in. For the first time, he confronts a chilling truth: He has no control over the events unfolding before him. The man who dominates the airwaves and speaks with authority now feels vulnerable and scared. Even worse, he must go inside and confront his wife, sharing a truth that will shatter her hopes. Given the current circumstances, there is little he can do to ensure their girls' safety.

Tony jumps into his car and drives to Nicole's house, ignoring the bright light illuminating the New York City skyline. He feels overwhelmed and sincerely wants to be with her through this difficult time.

What should have been a thirty-minute drive turns into a ninety-minute journey because of traffic and malfunctioning streetlights.

When he finally rings the doorbell, Nicole answers the door.

"Tony, it is good to see you! I'm scared. What on Earth is happening?"

Tony walks in and sits down on the couch.

"I don't know what's going on, either, but I knew I needed to be with you at this moment."

Nicole sits next to Tony. "This is crazy! We have no phone, internet, or TV service. There's no way to contact anyone or find out what's happening. I feel like I'm falling apart!"

Tony moves closer to Nicole and places his arm around her shoulders.

"Everything will be okay. I remember my mother telling me, 'This too shall pass' when things got rough. Honey, I believe we'll eventually find out why this is happening."

Tony gets up off the couch and looks around the house. "Where is Jason?"

"In the basement. Probably running old programs on his computer because he doesn't have internet service."

Tony walks to the basement door and shouts, "Jason, can you come up here for a moment?"

Nicole looks curiously at Tony. "What's going on?"

Tony stands by the basement door, waiting for Jason.

"Sweetheart, just be patient. You'll see."

Minutes later, Jason arrives upstairs.

"Yes, Mr. Stravell?"

"Your mother once told me that you keep nearly everything from your childhood."

"True that, Mr. Stravell."

Tony places his hand on Jason's shoulder.

"Listen, Jason, as you know, we have no internet, no TV, no phone, and no music. Do you still have your old CD player or AM/FM radio downstairs? It would really help us take our minds off things if you could find it and play some music."

Jason smiles. "You know, Mr. Stravell, I do have my old player and some cool CDs. Give me a little time to find them."

About an hour later, Jason comes upstairs again. He sets up his CD player and takes a seat on the couch across from Tony and Nicole. As smooth jazz plays, the living room's atmosphere lightens.

Tony looks at Nicole and smiles. "You see, Nicole, many people discarded their old stereo systems for internet streaming, thinking that streaming technology was the future. Now look at us, using CD players to entertain ourselves."

Tony shakes his head.

"My mother would have laughed at us if she could see us sorting through old stuff for CDs, or even worse, cassette tapes."

As smooth jazz plays throughout the room, Jason suddenly jumps up from the couch. "Mom, did you hear that?"

Nicole looks at Jason. "Hear what?"

Jason looks at his mother. "I heard a voice."

Nicole looks at Jason, and he can tell that she does not believe him.

"No, Mom, I'm serious! I heard a voice!"

Confused, Nicole looks at Jason.

"I always knew you were smoking weed downstairs, but I should have stopped it before you started hearing things!"

Jason, knowing precisely what he has heard, stares at his mother and says nothing as she continues to reprimand him for what he knows is true.

Meanwhile, Tony sits quietly on the couch, ignoring their conversation and trying to absorb everything around him. He's always believed that what his audience sees is what the establishment wants them to see, and it's his duty to uncover hidden truths. But this catastrophic disruption in the sky is different. There's no way to know the truth behind the mysterious light. He's assured Nicole and Jason that everything will be fine; however, he is putting on a brave face and has no idea what will happen next.

Seeing the ominous light filter through the curtains, Tony reluctantly admits that some things are better left unrevealed. Perhaps uncovering what lies beneath the surface could show something the people of this nation are not prepared for. His thoughts contradict every principle of his podcast, yet his feelings reflect his confusion and fear about what lies ahead.

As he watches Nicole and Jason argue, a smile creeps onto his face as he realizes that life is more than just hosting podcasts and debating politics; it's about relationships. A wave of sadness washes over him as he realizes it took a potential disaster for him to learn what truly matters in life.

Paul, with his family, gazes in disbelief at the light from their balcony. He cannot help but stare at the sky, wondering if he has hosted his last radio show. Turning to Kelly, he sees tears streaming down her face as she struggles to understand what she's witnessing. Paul grabs Kelly's hand, comforting her as they stare at the light.

Seeking understanding, Paul looks across the balcony at his boys and reflects on his life and career. He begins to question who his actual opponent in life is. He wonders whether his real challenge stems from the political opposition on the right or from a much larger enemy quietly hiding in the shadows. Perhaps all the political rhetoric and debates that have dominated talk radio for the last twenty years have masked the real, urgent threat facing humanity. It is a question that has troubled Paul throughout the evening.

As Preston and Pierce stand on the other side of the balcony, looking up at the light, Preston turns to Pierce and whispers, "Pierce, did you hear that?"

Pierce looks at his brother. "Hear what?"

Preston looks concerned. "The voice."

Pierce looks at Preston curiously. "What voice?"

Preston shrugs his shoulders. "Just forget it."

Frustrated, Pierce looks at Preston and grabs his arm. "No! Why didn't I hear it?"

Preston shrugs his shoulders while nervously looking up at the sky. "I don't know."

As anxiety surges through Pierce's mind, he glares at Preston.

"Well, what are you waiting for? What did the voice say?"

Preston freezes with anguish etching its way across his face. He hears Pierce's question but takes a moment to gather his thoughts. As he turns to his brother, the once-bright light in the sky fades, casting a dark shadow over the Earth's horizon.

Frightened, Pierce turns to Preston and shouts, "Preston! What did the damn voice say?"

Distressed, Preston catches his brother's eye and repeats the words he's heard from the light: "The time has come!"

20
Reflections

As the blazing light retreats from the Earth's atmosphere and heads toward the vastness of the universe, a conversation unfolds between two entities.

Entity One: "Where were you? We summoned you, but you didn't answer, so we sent out a universal signal, hoping you would hear it."

Entity Two: "I heard it, but I had to clean up a mess that was left behind."

Entity One: "You mean the mess that you left behind!"

A sense of unease hangs in the air as no words are exchanged.

Entity One: "So, you decided to disobey a direct order and felt compelled to alert them despite the council's warnings. You could not just leave them alone. You embarked on a covert mission, slipped through their portal, transformed into one of them, and interfered with their elections."

Entity Two: "Being part of their political structure was the only way I could gain enough authority to stop them from transmitting."

Entity One: "How did that work out for you? You infiltrated their system to prevent them from interacting with the unknown world, yet you failed, believing the researcher would take your warning seriously. Now, the disobedience of a single being has placed the entire planet in peril."

Entity Two: "You are right. But instead of watching another planet being destroyed, shouldn't we try to warn them? Their intentions are good, but their efforts to contact other worlds have put them in grave danger."

Entity One: "That I understand. If we can locate their signal, I assure you that others in our quadrant who are less friendly will note their coordinates and also make contact."

Entity Two: "Is there anything else we can do?"

Entity One: "You have done enough! We have seen planets rise and fall, but I will admit this one is unique in its composition and humanity. If its inhabitants can avoid self-destruction and work together, they might find a way to escape the fate that has befallen others. Perhaps our presence in their atmosphere will motivate them to succeed where we failed."

Entity Two: "By the way, there was no need to cut off all communications on the planet when you sent the signal to locate me. You know our universal frequency is transmitted on the first harmonic, so unfortunately, all firstborn species on the planet recognized your call. It was an unnecessary action that frightened many people."

Entity One: "If that frightened them, they better be prepared for what is to come. Like us, they need to understand they are not alone in the universe. By awakening certain forces through their transmissions, they will eventually encounter the same adversary we faced. Let us hope they handle it better than we did."

There is a moment of silence as they recall the plundering of their planet.

"Now, we have spent enough time focusing on them. We have our own planet to rebuild."

The following day, confusion and chaos erupted worldwide as billions of people sought answers about the mysterious light and its disappearance. The National News Center airs a special report on this terrifying event for its viewers.

"This is the National News Center, bringing you an emergency broadcast from our New York newsroom. After twenty-four hours of terror in the skies, the ominous light that caused worldwide fear and anxiety has finally vanished. All communication services are now back online, and countries around the globe are working to restore some measure of normalcy. However, government officials and authorities have no updates on the origin or disappearance of the anomaly. Even more concerning, Congress remains unaware of the president's whereabouts. We'll provide additional information as it becomes available."

Despite the unprecedented circumstances, Mitch arrives at his Manhattan studio and finds a concerned, shaken Jake preparing for the show. He remains silent as he sits at his desk, contemplating how to start the broadcast.

"Ladies and gentlemen, we have endured a harrowing experience in the past twenty-four hours. I have no answers regarding what we just went through, and I cannot predict whether it will happen again. Throughout my life, light has symbolized positivity and enlightenment; however, now it haunts me and millions of others as night falls upon our nation. I cannot provide you with any comfort for what you experienced yesterday, except to encourage you to hold on to your faith and pray."

Jake nods as he watches Mitch through the glass.

"If what we experienced yesterday was beyond our control, then we must turn to a God who is in control. Today, we'll steer clear of political and cultural discussions. Instead, let us take this time to reflect on the present and the blessings we currently have."

Jake stands up on the other side of the glass and signals for a break.

"Before we take a break, I want to express my gratitude to God that my daughters are safe and doing well. My wife and I were worried when we couldn't reach them. However, early this morning, we received confirmation that they are all right."

Mitch's eyes well up with tears as he continues.

"Ladies and gentlemen, this is Mitch Corvane, and I ask you to stay with us as we continue our coverage. We'll be right back."

Across town, Paul sits in his broadcast booth, still stunned by what he witnessed from his balcony. With his head bowed in silence, he remains lost in thought. Knowing him well, Rochelle decides to let him be.

Minutes later, Paul finally lifts his head and glances across the booth, giving Rochelle a nod. She presses a button on the control board, putting him on the air.

"Family, I don't know what to say after last night. How can there ever be any sense of normalcy after experiencing something like that? There's a humbling that comes over a person when they see their world and their family falling apart, feeling completely helpless. It's an emotion I never want to experience again."

Rochelle nods.

"I was on the balcony when the lights in the sky suddenly went out. I could hear the screams and cries of people on the street from my seventeenth-floor apartment. My two sons ran to me from the other end of the balcony, and as a family, we could do nothing but hold each other as the world seemed to end."

Rochelle looks at Paul with tears in her eyes.

"Forgive me for being completely honest, but I felt weak and less of a man as my family clung to me, trembling with fear. Just as abruptly as it had come, the light disappeared, and all forms of communication resumed. It was as though nothing had happened. But I know what I saw! Something happened, and everything has changed."

Rochelle calls for a break as Paul continues.

"Ladies and gentlemen, I don't know what the future holds, but I'm determined to savor every moment with family and friends. Stay tuned. We'll be back after this brief break."

As the sun sets on the Manhattan skyline, *The Gray Forum* starts.

"Good evening, my name is Tony Stravell, and I'm glad to be alive, hosting the number one podcast in the nation."

Tony pauses, reflects on everything that happened, and shakes his head in disbelief.

"What a night! As I sat at home with my girlfriend, now my fiancée, I realized what is truly important in life."

Tony slowly leans back in his chair.

"I have always been curious about everything since I was a young boy, including the belief that we're not alone in this universe. Last night, I experienced something that felt like validation of that belief. You can't convince me that something or someone didn't invade our space. I don't care what the government will say when they address the nation later this evening."

A frustrated Tony looks at Rob as he continues.

"We saw the light with our own eyes and witnessed something that not only warned this nation of an impending catastrophe but also placed the entire world on notice! I'm a proponent of transparency, but maybe, just maybe, some things need to remain in the dark. I know this goes against everything I have been advocating on my show. Yet if what happened last night is what I believe it to be, then it needs to stay hidden."

Tony reaches for his chair, lowers his voice, and takes his seat.

"As I sat in my fiancée's home, taking in the chaos happening in the sky, I realized what is important in the brief time we have on this planet. That is when I got on one knee, in front of her and her son, and proposed. It was not part of my initial intention, but drama has a way of shifting one's focus."

Rob signals for a break as Tony wraps up his monologue.

"*Gray Forum* family, I appreciate your support over the years. I don't know what the future holds, but I'm certain that something, or someone, holds our future. We'll be right back."

As evening settles in, Preston and Pierce stand on the balcony, watching the daylight transition into night. A sense of relief washes over them as they take in the breathtaking beauty of the stars.

Pierce glances at Preston as they gaze into the sky.

"It looks so peaceful and beautiful, so different from yesterday's chaos. Can you believe it?"

Preston glares at Pierce.

"I can believe anything now that we've witnessed what Mr. Sinclair did and the madness that came from the light."

There is an eerie silence as they continue to gaze at the stars. Then, a nervous Pierce turns to Preston. "Bro, why us?"

Preston, still captivated by the beauty of the stars, wonders what Pierce is talking about. "What do you mean?"

Grasping the magnitude of what they experienced at the research center, Pierce says, "Why are we the only ones who know what really happened? We didn't even tell Dad."

Preston, still gazing at the heavens, shrugs his shoulders. "I don't know."

Pierce, unsettled with Preston's response, says, "Do you think they will come back?"

Preston turns to Pierce with a concerned look on his face. "They already know we exist. They'll be back."

Pierce is disturbed by this response. "Bro, Dad was right! We need to educate ourselves and get ready."

Preston curiously stares at Pierce. "Ready for what?"

Pierce paces on the balcony, gazing up at the multitude of stars scattered across the sky.

"For their return!"

The End.

Please take a moment to share your thoughts by leaving a brief review on Amazon and any platform that features book reviews. Your insights provide invaluable feedback and support for this book, encouraging fellow independent writers to pursue their creative visions. Remember to avoid spoilers when discussing the story.

Thank you in advance for being a part of this journey!

Ken Bosket

About the Author

B orn in the projects of New York City, Ken Bosket, MSEM/Engr., transformed life's challenges into a foundation for purpose and success. A lifelong thinker, Bosket has consistently questioned societal norms, probing whether today's prevailing mindsets can sustain tomorrow's rapidly evolving, high-tech culture.

As he navigated the tension between personal ambition and spiritual conviction, his curiosity deepened. That inquisitiveness ultimately compelled him to explore and critically examine the complex, often conflicting relationship between spirituality, technology, and humanity.

Bosket's journey began unexpectedly in 2018 when, without any formal writing background, he felt compelled to put his thoughts on paper. That debut effort became *Cooked on the Outside, Raw on the Inside: The Struggle to Wait on God's Timing*, a reflective work that marked the start of his voice. He continued exploring personal expression in 2020 with *In One Ear, Out the Other: Hearing "The Word" in a Microwave Society*, further refining his narrative style. In 2023, Ken reached a new milestone with his premier work, *FLAWishing: Broken Yet Still Chosen*, a book that reflected his feelings in times of trouble and solidified his growth.

Never content to remain within a single genre, he later challenged himself creatively by venturing into political fiction with *Broadcast Blowout*: *Clash to the End*, demonstrating both versatility and a willingness to take risks.

To ensure his books remain accessible and engaging, Bosket developed a reader-friendly writing style that blends light-hearted conversation with insightful information and thought-provoking dialogue.

KENBOSKET.COM

KENBOSKET123@GMAIL.COM